SAMPSON TECHNICAL INSTITUTE

S0-BIZ-882

NORTH CAROLINA

ATION
LLEGES

LIBRARIES

BROKEN ACRES

PZ
7
B363
Br

BROKEN
ACRES

By Joyce Proctor Beaman

ILLUSTRATED BY MARY GOSLEN

JOHN F. BLAIR, Publisher
Winston-Salem, North Carolina

F
B

© 1971 BY JOHN F. BLAIR, PUBLISHER. ALL RIGHTS
RESERVED. LIBRARY OF CONGRESS CATALOG CARD
NUMBER: 72-156457. ISBN 0-910244-60-x.
PRINTED IN THE UNITED STATES OF AMERICA BY
HERITAGE PRINTERS, INC., CHARLOTTE, NORTH
CAROLINA.

7256

To My Son
BOBBY DAVID

ACKNOWLEDGMENTS

THE AUTHOR WISHES TO EXPRESS her appreciation to the following: Judy Webb, who struggled with the handwritten first copy in order to create a readable rough draft; Laura Bynum Wade, who typed the manuscript sent to the publisher; Dr. Robert Pope, who verified Teddy's ear problem; Mrs. Elizabeth Swindell, Mrs. Bernice Kelly Harris, Joe Eagles, Alton Boswell, George Thomas Daniel, Jim Fulghum, Thad Stem, Jr., John W. Beaman, L. H. Fountain, and Mr. and Mrs. Jesse Proctor, the author's parents, who read the manuscript prior to publication and made suggestions.

BROKEN ACRES

The characters in this book are fictitious. Any similarity to persons living or dead is purely coincidental. Only the setting, Wilson County, and the facts related to it are authentic. The time is the early nineteen–fifties.

CHAPTER 1

MELODY SAT ON THE DOORSTEP, poking lazily with a tobacco stick at a little patch of isolated wire grass. She had kicked off her sandals and with her big toe was playfully interrupting a line of the tiniest, brownish-red ants that formed an extended army along a narrow path leading to the wire grass. Finally, not being able to endure the silence any longer, she looked around at her father. "Getting too dark to read, Papa?"

"I reckon so. But how can anyone concentrate on a newspaper with such a sunset to enjoy?"

"I think it's the prettiest one ever, but I always think that. Maybe it's so pretty because it's Sunday. Everything does look and feel different on Sunday—the air, the sky, and everything—don't you think, Papa?"

"Well, in a way, I reckon. That red sunset means fair weather and an early start putting in tobacco tomorrow," teased Mr. Nottoman, knowing how much Melody hated to get up in the morning.

"Oh, Papa, did you have to mention that? But I'm depending on the frogs. Just listen to them—crying for rain."

Mr. Nottoman smiled.

1

Library

Sampson Technical Institute

"If I ever leave Big Oaks," said Melody, eager to change the subject, "I think I'll miss the old front porch and the sunset most of all."

She paused for a moment.

"No, Papa, I was just teasing because you teased me about getting up so early to put in tobacco. I'd miss you the most, along with Mama and Buster and Teddy and Pup-Pup-Too-Boy." When Pup-Pup heard his name, he opened his sleepy eyes and looked up at her, wagging his tail lazily. Melody patted him gently. "I reckon I'd just plain miss everything."

"Oh, you've a long time to stay around yet—twelve years already and many more to come."

Melody looked closely at her father. Even in the twilight, she noticed the slight graying of his dark-brown hair, not so curly as it used to be and somewhat thinner. Melody thought he was aging too fast. Farm work was strenuous and, especially in spring and summer, he always lost weight. She knew that he didn't weigh nearly the 175 pounds that he had a few years ago. Even when he had on his white Sunday shirt, the deep wrinkles in his tanned face made him look older than his forty-five years. Now he was rubbing the palms of his large, calloused hands back and forth on the ends of the arms of the chair. Melody noticed a faraway look in his usually contented blue eyes.

"Worried, Papa?"

"Oh, no. Why?"

"Just wondering."

Melody looked at her father for a moment.

"Papa, do you worry about Teddy?"

"Oh, yes, Melody, all of us do."

"Me, too, Papa. He's some four-year-old, isn't he? Sometimes he's thirty-three pounds of trouble, but the kind of trouble I enjoy."

Mr. Nottoman nodded his head in agreement.

Teddy was the youngest of the Nottoman family, with blond, curly hair and blue eyes—a bundle of energy and noise, full of curiosity, demanding answers and attention from every direction.

"Papa, you know something that bothers me? I hate to say it, but I'm kind of jealous of Teddy because he can sleep late in the mornings and I can't!"

"No, Melody, you're not really jealous. But have you ever thought what that obsession about sleeping late could amount to if you'd just change it into something good?"

Mr. Nottoman didn't know, but there was a secret obsession that Melody carried deep in her heart—to do something about Teddy's deformed ear. There was no visible opening of his left ear. In fact, there was no ear at all, just a small piece of jumbled, muffled skin where the ear ought to be. She had heard her mother explain to her father soon after Teddy was born that there wasn't much the doctors could do about it yet. Tests had proved that Teddy could hear with his right ear. His left ear might be fixed by a special operation, but there were no doctors in Wilson who could perform the surgery. It would be extremely expensive to take Teddy away from home and stay with him while he was recovering. Besides, an operation might be risking total deafness. Melody thought of what that would mean— no school like other boys and girls enjoyed, no sounds of laughter, no birds' songs. If he ever got lost, he couldn't even hear the calls of those searching for him.

But she thought she could bear everything if it were not for the pain. When Teddy had an earache, he pulled his ear until it was as red as fire and cried pitifully until the pain medicine took effect.

"Why did this have to happen to Teddy?" Melody asked herself. "If only it had been me. Someday I'll find a way. I declare I will!"

"What was that, Melody?"

"What, Papa?"

"What you're going to find a way to do."

"Just thinking, Papa, about Teddy."

"I guess it's normal for you to worry, Honey, but you must let me do the worrying about this. O.K?"

4

Melody knew she must not make her father worry about her because she worried. Right now, she must change the subject, even if it bothered her not to let him know her true thoughts. "Teddy is going to be all right, Papa. Wait and see!"

"You're just like your mother, Melody, always looking on the bright side."

"You know, I'd like to be more like Mama. Little and quiet, but so strong and sincere. She says I'm like you, all but my hair. But I'd like to be like her. . . . No, that's not right at all, Papa. I really want to be like the best of both of you."

"You're a mess, Melody."

Melody ran her right hand underneath the black hair that lay in loose curls just to her shoulders. She pulled it up against the back of her head, pretending to let the back of her neck cool. Every Saturday night when she removed the rubber band to free her ponytail, she chuckled to herself that all good ponies and ponytails must rest on Sunday.

Mrs. Nottoman opened the screen door and came from the living room to the porch. She was not more than five feet tall and still looked much younger than her thirty-eight years. Melody thought she had what the advertisements called a peaches-and-cream complexion. This, with her brown eyes and auburn hair, provided a picture that almost everyone around Big Oaks called pretty. And when she spoke, her voice was gentle and peaceful.

"I'd say you two are talking up a blue breeze out here."

"Oh, no, Mama. No breeze."

"Maybe I should say talking up a storm instead."

"Now that sounds more hopeful. If we have a storm and lots of rain, we can't put in tobacco tomorrow, can we, Papa?"

"I doubt it, but we'll see. Just in case we do, you'd better get to bed early and get some rest, don't you think?"

"You're right, Papa. It's not quite bedtime, but I have a few things to do in my room before I go to sleep. 'Night, Mama. 'Night, Papa. See you in the morning, but not too early, I hope."

Melody went to her room with thoughts of tobacco and Teddy still on her mind. Before she closed the door, she turned on the small table lamp beside her bed. A slight breeze had risen and fluttered the white organdy curtains, causing them to cast dancing shadows against the yellow walls. Immediately, she went to her dressing table, lifted the yellow cover, and took out her little red flashlight. As soon as she could brush her hair, dress for bed, turn out the light, and be sure that her parents were asleep, she would get out the little white-cloth

6

sugar sack. It had been several days since she had checked it, and she was eager to see it again.

Her mother came in from the porch and went to her room. Melody knew that her father had gone to check the barns and livestock, as he always did before going to bed. Suddenly Teddy cried out. Melody heard him going toward the kitchen, where he knew his mother kept his medicine.

Melody reached the kitchen about the same time as Mrs. Nottoman. Teddy was whining and pulling his ear. Melody picked him up and held him close to her chest. He flung his legs around her waist and his arms around her neck, laying his hot cheek against her face.

His mother melted the pain tablet in a spoon containing orange juice and gave it to him. "There now. We're going to feel better in just a minute."

After they got Teddy back to his room, Melody laid him gently in bed. His hair was damp and his neck was warm. Melody felt his forehead. It, too, was warm. Always, when the ear pained, he seemed to have a little fever, but with aspirin and pain medicine, he soon got all right. Melody wondered if he would tonight.

After a few minutes Melody said quietly, "I'll stay in his room for a while, Mama. I don't mind. In fact, I really want to. I'll be a good nurse."

"O.K., if you insist, but call me if you need me."

Melody looked at Teddy and then, craving a breeze,

tiptoed to the window. Nothing was there now except the hot, sultry stillness of a dark summer night.

She listened to Teddy's breathing. When he went to sleep, he would breathe differently by blowing through his lips, making a puffing sound, as if he were blowing out a candle.

While waiting for Teddy to fall asleep, she remembered Mama and the way she looked in the kitchen, just as pretty in her powder-blue housedress as she did in her Sunday best. She wondered if Mama's worrying about Teddy had caused her hair to turn gray. In an old almanac, she had read something about worry and gray hair. Melody wished she wouldn't worry. She knew that Mama would give her life to see Teddy's ear healed, but no amount of motherly sacrifice could help. It would take a doctor—a good one.

Teddy was blowing bubble sounds now. Melody went to his bed, bent over, kissed him good night, and whispered something about loving him. She, too, must get some sleep. Tomorrow would come too soon. But before she could sleep, there was one more important thing she had to do. She must check the white-cloth sugar bag.

Back in her room, she immediately closed the door and turned out the light. Papa and Mama must not hear or see her. She laid the flashlight on the bed underneath the top sheet, and carefully untucking it from the mattress, she lifted the bottom sheet. Then she knelt on the floor beside the bed. The neat stitches made with Papa's large, plantbed-canvas needle still held. Melody untied the knot at one end and removed the string.

"Oh," she thought, "if Mama saw this tear in the mattress—this rip!" But the rip had come there naturally, soon after she was ten and big enough to have a room of her own. Sometime when she was late for school and Mama made her bed, perhaps she had noticed the stitches; and at cleaning time, when Buster and Papa took the mattress outside to sun, she worried about them finding the stitches.

She reached inside the rip and pulled out the sugar sack with the letters still on it. Always, when she opened it, the paper bag inside rattled a little, and she had to be extra careful as she reached inside so that she wouldn't make enough noise to wake or disturb Mama and Papa. The coins and bills were still there. It was too hot to count them tonight, but it was reassuring to know that they were still safe. She removed the half-piece of notebook paper and read quickly by flashlight: ice-cream money saved—$16.80; picking up pecans—$.35; gift from Aunt Sue—$2.00; found on the school ground and unclaimed—$.50; sale of rabbit's foot to Buster—$.10; change from the school play that Papa said I could keep —$.15. Total: $19.90. There could have been a little more, but sometimes, ice cream just couldn't be resisted, especially on those warm spring days. But she had said that ten days with ice cream was the absolute limit. And the lunchroom meal was always enough. It was hard, though, to resist ice cream when the other boys and girls were eating. But there were those who didn't eat because they didn't have a dime and couldn't get it. Their parents, many of whom were farmers, did not have it to give.

Papa had said that when they got to be ten years old, they were half-grown and it was time to start saving for an education. It was agreed that each year she and Buster would get the tips or final cropping from one acre of tobacco. In these years immediately after the Korean War, this would amount to about $200.00 each. This was to be used for school clothes, school fees, school supplies, and of course, the tithe. If any was left, it was to be put into the bank to draw interest and used later to pay for an education. That was essential, but Melody longed to see the fulfillment of a more important dream—doing something about Teddy's ear. The little sugar bag could help, she hoped.

She put the sugar bag back in the mattress. Sewing up the ripped seam would have to wait until tomorrow. There was too much risk now of pricking her finger with the big needle. Maybe it could be done during the noon-hour rest period.

She turned off the flashlight and crawled into bed,

but she could not go to sleep. Suppose they did hear of a doctor who could do something for Teddy's ear and they had a crop failure and couldn't pay the other debts? She knew that some food was grown on the farm, but much had to be bought. There were crop expenses —seed, fertilizer, labor to harvest it, and curing oil, as well as machinery payments each year and essential repairs on the house and farm buildings. Money circulated in the fall, but it went from Papa's hand to someone else's—to pay debts or to pay back borrowed money. Money always got very low just before Christmas until some could be borrowed from the bank at the beginning of the year. That lasted pretty well, if spent wisely, until more could be borrowed in late June to harvest the crop. One always had to borrow money from the borrowed money. Most of the farmers lived like this. Some of the farmers raised hogs, but often hogs had cholera and died. Some raised corn, but it often had to be sold at the market at low prices in early fall, because most of the farmers could not afford to keep it until prices rose in the spring. There was no getting ahead.

Even though Papa owned his land, in good years they always had less than $1,200.00 left when all the debts were paid. This had to last until the next fall—to be supplemented with borrowed money.

So where would they ever get the money for Teddy's

ear if they ever found a doctor? Suppose the doctor died or moved to another state before they could afford to take Teddy to him? Suppose he required a big down payment before he would even start on an operation or treatment? They could sell the farm or mortgage it, but it would take years to replace the money.

"If you think something good long enough and hard enough, you can make it come true," Melody whispered. Excitedly, she turned on her flashlight, reached for a pencil and paper on the table beside her bed, and began to add: $75.00 saved when ten years old; $101.00 at age 11; $19.90 in the sugar bag; total already saved: $195.90. This year, if the tips were good, she could perhaps save a little more, maybe $125.00. She did not need many clothes. The warehouseman had given her some advertising pencils and large note pads—this saved pencil and paper money. And ice-cream money— 180 days at 10c per day.

Let's see, $195.90, plus $125.00, plus $18.00, equals $338.90, she figured quickly. That's enough to offer any doctor in the beginning. That was a start! That was it! She couldn't lose now!

But suppose the crop failed as it had three years ago —the year before the college-fund idea was started. There would be no tip money, no ice-cream money, no money to add to the fund. But it couldn't happen. It just couldn't.

Rainfrogs still sang in the distance, making a noise like the sound of wet pebbles being rubbed together. "I could stay up all night and never get sleepy. I could sleep day and night, but I'd still hate to get up in the morning, especially to work in tobacco," Melody thought aloud. "But it is our only hope for money and for Teddy—except for the secret sugar-bag treasure."

The night air was thick and heavy. Melody, hoping a breeze would blow through her room as it had earlier in the night, got up to open the door that led to the hall. Her parents' room was on the other side of the hall. Their door was open, and Melody wondered whether they had been able to go to sleep.

After she lay down again, she heard them talking. Often, they talked about Teddy when they could not go to sleep, but this time it was not Teddy. It was the airport problem. Her father sounded troubled. So did her mother.

"They're talking about locating it somewhere in this county. It's as likely as not to be right here in this vicinity. Some men were doing some scouting and talking," Mr. Nottoman was saying.

Melody's face flushed. Her heart beat heavily. "They couldn't. They just couldn't take Big Oaks and all the small surrounding farms and turn them into one big, flat airport," she said to herself.

Now her father was saying something about answer-

13

ing one of those ads describing farms for sale in Virginia, just in case they had to move.

Everybody thought it had been assured that the airport would not be located near Big Oaks. But evidently, her father knew something new. Where would everybody go? Would they burn the houses or tear them down or just move them away? But there was nowhere to move them.

Melody closed her eyes. She could see it now: miles of cement, big shelters, rows of office buildings, and garages—but no farms, no homes, no fields, no woods; just a plain cement desert as far as anyone could see—not even a marker to say, "This once was Big Oaks."

Her parents had stopped talking. For a few moments, Melody lay very still, completely confused and frustrated, as her eyelids became heavier and heavier. Tiny hot tears oozed from her eyes and ran down the sides of her face, dropping into her ears. The tears seemed to offer the relief she needed, and she fell asleep at last.

CHAPTER 2

"MELODY! MELODY JANE NOTTOMAN!" roared Buster's voice through the crisp morning air.

Melody did not stir. The house was quiet except for the rattling of a few dishes as Mrs. Nottoman hurriedly prepared breakfast.

"Mel-o-dee! You heard Papa say yesterday that we were gonna get started as early as we could before the tobacco flops," Buster yelled.

Melody turned over in bed and pulled the sheet over her head. "Tobacco, tobacco, tobacco," she mumbled.

Melody knew that Buster's chief joy was getting her out of bed, especially on tobacco-barning days. She was aware that this was one way he had of getting even with her for all her teasing about his red hair and freckles. He had told her that it was a good thing she was a girl, or they would settle their differences in a sure way. Just having reached sixteen, he had talked his father into signing for him to get a driver's permit. Melody declared that this had ruined him for sure. He had admitted that he would almost rather not have it if she was going to tease him about girls. Even when he said that he didn't want a license so that he could drive to

15

see girls, that he just wanted to drive the farm truck to take tobacco to the market and to do other farm chores, she pretended not to believe him.

"Melody, Papa told me to come and call you. This is the last time I'm gonna call."

"But, Buster, I'm sleepy."

"Oh, you're sleepy, are you? This is just the second week of putting in tobacco, and here you're complaining as if you'd been worked to death. What'll you be saying by the end of six weeks?"

Melody realized that she was fighting a losing battle. As she ran her long, slender fingers through her tousled hair, she mumbled something to herself about never marrying a farmer. She dropped her feet to the floor, her eyes still closed. She leaned over, fell back on the bed, and was fast asleep again. A moment later the alarm clock sounded. She jumped to her feet with her usual startled response. "I'll never marry a farmer. I never, never will. I'll never make the same mistake that Pocahontas made by marrying John Rolfe."

"Melody Jane, do I hear you talking?"

"Yes, Mama, just talking to myself. I'll be in there in a minute. Do you know where Papa is?"

"He's in the tobacco patch. Just went out to see if it's ripe enough to crop."

Melody ran to the window. The sun was just beginning to blaze red behind the treetops. "Going to be a hot day! Gee, I dread it." She breathed deeply.

"Papa! Papa! Where are you? I want to talk with you!" she yelled out the window. Then she stretched on her tiptoes to see if she could catch a glimpse of her father, but the tobacco was so tall and overlapped in the rows so closely that she could not see him.

She caught one last deep breath of fresh air, turned around, and tiptoed to Teddy's room. He was sleeping soundly. She laid her hand gently against his forehead. It felt normal. The medicine had stopped the pain once again. She wondered how he could sleep with all the noise Buster had been making.

"When it comes to sleeping, he's plenty kin to me, bless his heart." Melody chuckled as she ran toward the kitchen.

"Good morning, Mama. How are you on this *nice* Monday?"

"Melody Nottoman. You haven't even dressed. What on earth have you been doing?"

"Mama, I wish God had made Monday a rest day so we could rest from Sunday!"

"Oh, Melody!"

"And, Mama, you know something. I'm not going to marry a farmer. I'm going to marry a preacher. Then I can sleep all day long on Monday."

"Preachers and preachers' wives have to work, too, you know."

"You're right, Mama. I was joking. Are you sure Papa's in the tobacco patch? I couldn't see him a minute ago. The way that tobacco's growing, we'll be putting in until Halloween. Bet there are thirty leaves to a stalk. Can't even miss the first cropping last week."

"Melody! Have you forgotten what a time we had resetting it six weeks ago and the chopping and plowing and suckering? You'd better be thankful for every leaf."

"I am, Mama; really I am. I just hate to get up so early on Monday morning—just because of tobacco. Before I peel the potatoes, may I check with Papa? He might not be going to put in today," continued Melody, sticking a hole in a warm biscuit and filling it with black molasses.

"Melody Nottoman! What did you ask? And where are you going in your nightgown?"

"I'll be back in a minute. Honest Injun!"

Melody ran across the dew-covered grass, her uncombed hair and yellow gingham nightgown flying in the breeze. "Papa, Papa! Where are you?"

"Over here by the apple tree," yelled Mr. Nottoman.

Melody ran down the rows of tobacco. Because of the morning dew, the tobacco was not so gummy as usual, but as she passed by, her nightgown became wetter and wetter. From time to time, drops of gummy dew splashed into her eyes, burning them and making her stop to squinch them or wipe them with her nightgown. Wet and breathing hard, she found Mr. Nottoman.

"Melody, are you crazy? Out here in your nightgown —and barefooted! This dew and damp air will give you your death of cold. And your wet clothing, it's sticking tight to you. Here, put on my raincoat."

"I'm sorry, Papa. I just wanted to make sure you were going to put in tobacco before I dressed. If you aren't, I'm going back to bed and sleep all day. Tell me, Papa, is it ripe enough to put in?"

"Melody Nottoman. You *are* crazy. You can't go back to bed in those clothes!"

"Well, Papa, I forgot about the dew. Everybody forgets something sometimes."

"Oh, yes, but there are certain important things that we must not forget, little friend!"

"I know, Papa. I'll do better next time. Listen, Papa, I believe I hear Jake coming down the road with the mule and tobacco truck. Isn't it funny how sounds carry so far in the morning?"

Jake Binger was Mr. Nottoman's right-hand man. Having lived on the Nottoman farm for many years, he and his family helped the Nottomans tend and harvest most of the crops.

Melody climbed on top of a barrel left in the field from planting season, one of those used for refilling the transplanter with water. "It *is* Jake. And Little Moses is with him. You know something, Papa. I think it's plum pitiful to get growing children up so early just to put in tobacco!"

"There are a lot of things worse than getting up early."

Melody climbed off the barrel, paused, stood on her tiptoes, reached up and broke a flowering top from a hill of tobacco. "Well, that's one that won't turn into seed," she said. "Listen, Papa, the noise of the tobacco truck is getting louder. Old Kate must be running away! Let's go see, Papa!"

Melody and her father ran across the rows of big, green tobacco, pushing stalks to this side and that side to open the way.

"Look, Papa. Old Kate *is* running away. She's already thrown Jake from the truck. Look, he's in the ditch!"

Jake was bleeding from a deep gash in his face. He covered his black face with his hands and cried, "My boy, my boy! Git Little Moses. Don't let him fall from dat truck an' git killed!"

"Are you hurt much, Jake?"

"Naw, suh, not much. Git Little Moses!"

Melody and her father ran to the yard and jumped into the truck. As usual, it was slow in starting. "Dear God, please!" begged Melody. "Look, Papa. Little

20

Moses and Old Kate are 'way down the road. Hurry, Papa!"

Mrs. Nottoman came to the door to ask what was happening. Mr. Nottoman yelled quickly that Old Kate had run away and that Little Moses might be hurt. They'd be back as soon as they could.

Old Kate had run into the ditch, pulling the tobacco truck behind her. Little Moses had fallen off. When they stopped, Melody ran to him. He was lying face down, his feet in the ditch, his head on the highway. She bent over and turned his face up. "Oh, no, Papa. Look! He got his throat caught by a nail in one of the truck rounds. Look at the blood just pouring out. He's bleeding to death. He must have put up one of the truck rounds to hold by. Look, Papa. He looks so funny. I think he's dead!"

Mr. Nottoman packed the wound with gauze from a first-aid kit he kept in the pocket of the truck. Melody ripped the tail from her nightgown, and they tied the nightgown tail firmly around Little Moses' neck to hold the gauze in place. Little Moses' head flopped backwards as Mr. Nottoman lifted him in his arms and carried him to the truck, and more blood oozed from the cut on his neck.

Jake was running toward them, with blood all over his face, his patched gray shirt, and his wash-worn

breeches. Even his bare feet were spotted with red. A short, stubby sort of man, he was panting like a run-out hound after a hunt.

When he got into the truck and saw his son, his trembling seemed to make the old truck shake, and he broke down and wept over Little Moses as if his heart would break.

"Lawd God, Mr. Nottoman. I ain't got nothin' but my chillen an' God comes along an' takes 'em. What is we gonna do? Lawd, Mr. Nottoman. Lawd, Lawd, Lawd. He's bleedin' to death. Look at him, Mr. Nottoman. He's bleedin' plum to death!"

Mr. Nottoman was driving as fast as he could toward Wilson. "There's no time to stop for his mama," he told Jake.

"Alice-Cora-Jane'll never forgive us. She ought to know 'bout Little Moses so she can at least pray for him," sobbed Jake. "But every split second counts gettin' him to de hospital."

"I'll hold his head, and you pray, Jake, not out loud, just pray," said Melody.

"I'm doin' dat, Miss Melody. Just sayin' words an' mo' words. Maybe de good Lawd will put 'em together."

Jake reached to the foot of the truck, took an old piece of tobacco canvas, and wiped his bloody face.

Melody saw that the gashes were not deep. She was worried about Jake's getting an infection from the tobacco canvas, but she was more worried about Little Moses' life. She felt his cheek. It was still warm. She felt for his pulse. She could feel nothing.

"Hurry, Papa. Hurry!"

The old truck was getting hotter and hotter. Burned oil on the motor filled the cab with a pale blue smoke and a sickening odor.

Jake held Little Moses' hand and sat there with his eyes closed. Melody knew he was praying. Only once during the ten-mile drive to Wilson did he break the silence. "Mr. Nottoman, reckon dey wouldn't let us in at de white folkses' hospital? We gits to dat one first, you knows."

Mr. Nottoman did not answer. As he drove toward the hospital, he was hindered by the train, by the stoplights, and especially by other farmers hauling tobacco hands out of Wilson. It was still early, but the streets were already lined here and there with colored men, women, and children waiting to be asked to go to the farms to work. Horns honked. Farmers yelled to those standing on the street, asking them how much they'd charge to crop tobacco or loop or hand. Sometimes the hands got on the truck. Sometimes the farmers drove away.

At the hospital, all was quiet. Mr. Nottoman quickly found a nurse. She came out the back door with an orderly, who was pushing a stretcher.

Little Moses appeared dead. The orderly, a tall Negro with a white jacket and blue trousers, lifted him onto the stretcher. They took him to a little room. Two doctors and another nurse came around the corner and went quickly into the room where Little Moses was. Everyone moved efficiently, in spite of the many cold stares from the other patients in the emergency waiting room. Another nurse motioned to Melody and Jake to come to a small room across the hall. As they entered, she said, "They're looking after the little boy. We'd better check you."

She took a piece of cotton, put some liquid on it, and rubbed Jake's wound lightly. Even though it had bled profusely in the beginning, it was not deep and required no stitches. However, tiny drops of blood oozed forth as the gentle nurse wiped the old blood from the wound. In a few seconds she applied a red liquid that made Jake flinch. And then she bandaged the cuts.

Afterwards, Melody and Jake returned to the hall and sat on the bench, Jake in his blood-splotched clothes and Melody in her father's raincoat.

Jake sat with his head bowed. He was beginning to show every one of his fifty-one years. His stooped shoulders made his neck and head protrude and dip forward, so that he looked even shorter than his five-foot, two-inch frame. The deep lines in his dark face, worn by years of hard work and sacrifice, were now etched more deeply by sorrow. Not only his hair but also his eyebrows were beginning to turn gray.

Melody sat beside him, watching the patients going in and out of the emergency room and listening to the strange hospital noises.

Mr. Nottoman was still inside with the doctors, Little Moses, and the other nurse.

Two hours later they came out, and the doctor said a lot about stitches and blood transfusions and blood poisoning and oxygen. Jake and Melody listened. Jake twisted his faded brown-felt hat in his black hands.

Finally it was decided that Melody and Mr. Nottoman were to leave Jake at the hospital at least for that day, return home, and bring Alice-Cora-Jane to the hospital to be with Little Moses.

CHAPTER 3

IT WAS AFTER DINNERTIME before everything was settled at the hospital. Since the tobacco had flopped in the 99° temperature, Mr. Nottoman decided that he would wait until Tuesday morning to put in tobacco. However, he said that he and Buster and Jake's boys would break a few bottom suckers from the tobacco. He told them that he was worrying because the little sprouts were getting so large they were drawing the strength from the leaves.

"Mama, I don't mean to be critical. Really, I don't. But if it's too hot to put in tobacco, it seems that it's too hot for Buster and the others to sucker."

"Melody, your Papa loves his work and his land and his tobacco and the people who work for him. Seems to me you're suffering most of all. Come on, you've beans to pick and I've a chicken to kill for tomorrow's dinner."

"Mama, you always take up for Papa. You must love him or respect him or something," she teased. "But one thing always puzzles me. Why did you all have to settle down here to live where they grow tobacco? Just think, go twenty miles east and they raise peanuts; you can eat them. Go twenty miles west and they grow strawberries; you can eat them. Go twenty miles south and they grow cotton and corn; you eat corn and wear cotton. Go twenty miles north—just think of it—north—New York, where they have everything."

"Life is good according to what you make of it. You know the old saying about grass being greener on the other side of the fence."

"Yes, Mama. I know."

Teddy came around the corner of the house riding his tricycle—a faded blue one with broken spokes and wobbly wheels, inherited from Buster's boyhood days. "I'm going on a long trip, Melody—all around the house and back. See you later," he yelled as he disappeared around the corner of the house in a path well marked from previous trips.

Melody watched him disappear. She picked up the old brown vegetable basket and went to the garden. As she picked beans, she thought about Teddy. He had everything, it seemed, except his ear. No child could have more energy. He could climb the highest pasture fence, lift and carry a regular-size watermelon, or frolic all day and have more energy at dusk than at dawn. He could plant corn, like Papa, that would sprout and grow. Almost anywhere, one could find signs of his planting—beans in the flower garden, a stalk of corn at the back doorstep and another beside the well, flowers among the corn rows. His joy at yard-cleaning time was to load the trash in his red wagon and haul it to the trash pile. He asked millions of questions; and if he heard a new word, he'd say it over and over in a sing-song way until he seemed to master it. One of his favorite pastimes was making up the words of songs to fit tunes he knew. Somehow, the words usually came out right. Sometimes he declared that he was going to be a doctor like the ones that came to stick needles in Papa's hogs and cows. Sometimes he said he was going to be a garden-fixer like Mama. And when Buster cranked the farm truck, he thought he wanted to be a truck driver.

In tobacco season, it seemed that Teddy's ear was almost forgotten. Yet Melody knew that her parents never gave up hope. Nor did she. The tip money from the tobacco was part of the dream, part of the answer. She could not forsake this means for her hope to come true.

That night, bugs squeezed through the tiny holes in the window screen and almost covered Melody's bed before she could finish recording in her diary her special request. "Dear God, please help us find a doctor for Teddy's ear, and please help Little Moses to get well," she wrote as she remembered the message sent by Jake that Little Moses was getting weaker. Then she turned off the light and shook the sheet, dumping the little miseries on the floor, where they soon regained their strength and crawled again on her bed. A lone mosquito singing above her head joined the bug crew in their torture. She turned on the light, folded a piece of newspaper, and attempted to find the buzzing fiend. Her declaration of war was useless. The mosquito sat somewhere on his contented haunches refusing to budge, fly, or sing. Melody scratched and slapped and suffered. This was one of those nights.

Since she could not sleep, she considered going to the porch to talk with her father. She remembered that it was on a night like this last summer that he had told her so much about tobacco. She had been surprised to learn that one tobacco plant produced over a hundred and fifty thousand seeds—enough to plant a hundred square yards in a plant bed, which would furnish enough plants to set two to five acres of tobacco. She especially liked to hear him tell the love story of Pocahontas and John Rolfe and their interest in tobacco in the days when America was just beginning.

But remembering that she must get up before daybreak to help take the lugs from the barn to the packhouse, she decided not to join her father. That joy must wait. He would be coming in soon. She dreaded taking out sandlugs, all that dirt falling off the tobacco on her face and down her back. But six acres produced only about seven hundred sticks of first curings, so she comforted herself by saying that it shouldn't take long to take them out if there was enough moisture to soften them into good order so they would pack easily.

Drowsiness overcame Melody and, toward midnight, she fell asleep, only to be awakened before dawn by loud poundings on the back screen door. "Mr. Nottoman. Mr. Nottoman. Come here quick. Little Moses 'bout to die. Papa sent a man dat said Little Moses got to git some blood confusions quick or he gonna die. Papa Jake said for you to git somebody to git some blood confusions for Little Moses."

It was Abraham Binger, a little bit of a boy for a twelve-year-old. He was barefooted and wore no clothes except a dingy pair of faded brown trousers, which presented no contrast to his dark skin. Tiny ringlets of curly stiff black hair lay thick on the top of his head. Beads of sweat covered his forehead, and his big black eyes looked scared enough to have just viewed death itself.

When Melody and her father got to Abraham, Mr. Nottoman, sensing the boy's fear and desperation, said, "Melody, run quickly. Tell Mama to call the neighbors about giving blood. Ask them if they can be ready in five minutes. And you'd . . . no, better not bother Mr. Ezra about this."

Melody ran into the house. Her mother immediately appeared with her to find out what was happening. Mr.

Nottoman explained quickly and she went inside to call the neighbors.

"I bet you ran every step of the way, Abraham," Mr. Nottoman said. "Sit down here on the doorstep and rest a minute."

"Papa Jake says ever' minute is 'portant. Little Moses is dyin'. He's got to have some blood confusions in a heap hurry!"

"Blood *trans*fusions, Abraham. We know it's important. They're calling now," comforted Mr. Nottoman.

"Papa says dat Mama says dat Little Moses 'bout to die an' got to have some blood confusions, but dat if you can, she didn't want you to ask dat Mr. Ezra fo' no blood in her youngun. Might make him bad like Mr. Ezra. An' she said she 'bout as soon Little Moses be dead as be like Mr. Ezra."

"Did your mama say this or did you make it up, Abraham?"

"She said it to de man what come to tell Papa to tell me to come here an' tell you 'bout de blood confusions. I'd swear to it if I won't taught not to swear. I swear I'd swear to it."

"You're using mighty big words for a twelve-year-old. Your mama would be mighty upset if she heard you trying out those big words."

"Yas, suh. I knows—whopping upset, I 'spect."

Before sunrise, Mr. Nottoman and five neighbors

were on their way to Wilson, leaving Buster, Melody, and Abraham behind to take the cured tobacco out of the barn and start putting in.

As Melody and Abraham made their way down the dusty path to the tobacco barn, Abraham kicked the dirt, sending a little cloud swirling ahead. "You know somethin', Miss Melody? Dey didn't carry no blood with 'em, 'cause I looked ever' where when dey stopped to speak to Buster, an' dey sure didn't have none."

"What are you talking about, Abraham? They're carrying their blood in their bodies. And when they get to that big hospital in Wilson, they'll lay them on a table and take a big needle and draw out a whole jarful through a little tube."

"Sho' 'nough?"

"Sure enough, Abraham."

"How come you know so much, Miss Melody? You ever give blood?"

"No; Papa told me how it is."

"I thought somebody must've tol' you 'cause I didn't think you knowed so much jist natural."

"No, not much real knowledge is natural, Abraham. You've got to learn it from somewhere—from school or reading or from folks like Papa."

CHAPTER 4

BY THE TIME THE SUN SHOWED ITS FACE, one barn of dirty lugs had been carefully transferred to the packhouse. Three loads of green tobacco had been looped and hung in the racks shaded by broken branches from trees. Breakfast had come hurriedly somewhere in between.

Through the sultry air came the voices of the croppers in the nearby field yelling at the mules. The biting flies were worse than usual. They bit at the bare feet of Martha and Mary Binger, who handed tobacco to Melody as she looped it on the sticks.

Everyone was quiet. Quietness at a tobacco bench was unusual, but everyone was worried about Little Moses. Occasionally, Jacob and Joseph, seemingly unaware of their brother's danger, broke the silence as they played under the wild cherry tree beside the nearby barn.

"Barefeeted, barefeeted, barefeeted me,
   All aroun' dis cherry tree."

Jacob, almost six, and Joseph, ten months younger, thought of themselves as twins. They refused to wear shoes. They would stand side by side, one placing his foot against the other's to see which was longer, or measure their hands by clapping palm against palm and holding. They weighed on the cotton scales that Mr. Nottoman kept under the unused tobacco barn shelter. Jacob had once eaten a whole watermelon about the size of a ten-quart bucket just to weigh more than Joseph. He did for a few minutes, but he was sick the rest of the day.

"Jacob an' Joseph, you come here," commanded Mary. "One o' you can take one end o' dese sticks an' de other one can take de other end an' save me an' Martha a little trouble. 'Tain't right for us to work all de time an' y'all do nothin'. Come here!"

"We ain't big 'nough to work, Mary."

"Yes, you is. I sho' 'nough won't big as you when Mama Alice-Cora-Jane started me off workin'. Here. Take dis stick."

"We sho' 'nough is too little to work, an' we gonna tell Mama Alice-Cora-Jane."

"You's too little to 'member dat long. You'll be done forgot 'fore you sees her."

Reluctantly, Jacob and Joseph took the stick of looped tobacco with its long green leaves tied neatly on each side and hung it in the racks. Then, before Mary could give another command, they ran to the other barn and hid behind it.

36

"Look," shouted Melody, as she glanced toward the house. "It's Papa and Jake! Maybe they've got some news about Little Moses."

Jacob and Joseph came from behind the barn and ran to meet Jake, who was shuffling towards the tobacco bench while Mr. Nottoman moved the truck underneath the shade of one of the big oaks.

"He don't look so happy," said Martha, picking a tobacco worm from the hem of her gummy dress. "I bet Little Moses don't never git well."

"Don't say that, Martha. He will. I just feel it inside," said Melody, acknowledging a sense of guilt that she was hiding her true feelings. "How is Little Moses, Jake?"

"Can't say, Miss Melody. Got to wait fo' de blood transfusions to work. He sho' is a bad-lookin' young'un to me."

"The blood transfusions will help; I know they will," comforted Melody.

"Guess I better go to de field. Don' look like y'all needs no help up here. Been catchin' up dis mornin'?"

"Sometimes. Not often 'nough 'less it was all sit-down!" said Mary.

"You is too little to sit down—a 'leven-year-old talkin' 'bout bein' tired an' wantin' to sit down," said Jake quickly.

"But I is tired, Papa Jake. I sho' 'nough is."

Jake started to the field, seeming not to hear Mary's complaint. As soon as he was out of sight, Martha and Mary resumed their usual arguing.

"An' if you won't so skinny, you would be mo' able to work mo' better all de time," said Martha.

"An' if you won't so fat, you wouldn't git so tired so fast," answered Mary.

"Ain't Mary 'bout de prissiest person you ever seed? Ain't she now, Miss Melody? She's always twistin' an' turnin' an' jumpin' aroun' like a spring chicken."

"You's so fat you's like dead weight. You can't do nothin' but eat an' sleep an' git mo' fatter. Look how big yore face is—round an' fat. Look at yore nose an' dem big ears."

"When we catches up 'dis truck, we's gonna see who is best woman aroun' here, jist de two of us. I think I knows. I ain't lost yet, an' I don't plan to start now."

"You all ought to be ashamed fussing when your brother's so sick," said Melody.

Mary and Martha looked at each other and then at Melody. They seemed embarrassed.

"But she bothers me, Miss Melody."

"An' she bothers me, Miss Melody," echoed Mary.

"Well, if you bother each other, you're equal. O.K.?"

About ten o'clock the mailman stopped to leave the usual circulars and the daily paper. This broke the monotony of the morning's routine.

38

Mrs. Nottoman sent the circulars to the barn by Teddy. This gave him a feeling of importance, as one could easily see by his running and panting. "Here's de papers, Melody," he said with pride, believing that he had done a great service. He was so hot and out of breath that he sat down to cool on a cinder block under the shelter near Melody's looping rack. Melody looked at him and smiled. For a moment she was ashamed of herself for hating tobacco and hating to get up early. Teddy left his cinder block and joined the handers. Melody reached to get the bundle of tobacco that he had pulled from the truck, leaf by leaf. Instead of the required three leaves, he had six. Instead of all stems together, he had stems and tails mixed. Melody stopped to separate the bundle and arrange it acceptably. After all, children had to learn, she reasoned.

"Now I'm a tobacco-hander; but when I get big, I'm going to be a tobacco-picker like Papa."

"A what?" questioned Melody. She wondered where on earth he had heard that word. Everybody else said tobacco cropper or tobacco primer.

"You know Papa let me pick tobacco last week. I got too many leaves, he said, but I did get gum on my hands and hair and everything. I'm just about a big man like Papa, ain't I, Melody?"

And so, in spite of the heat and chatter, the work went on. About eleven o'clock Mr. Nottoman sent word to the bench by Aaron Binger, the truck driver, that the tobacco had flopped so much that everyone might as well stop for dinner.

As Melody walked to the house, eager to reach the shaded grove of tall oak trees that surrounded the Nottoman home, she saw Mr. Ezra Bowles, a neighbor, coming down the road in his smoking, coughing farm truck. Once black, it was now a mixture of purplish-blue from road smog, sunshine, hog-hauling, field dirt, and general unconcern on Mr. Ezra's part. Beaten, bruised, bent, and battered from general use, it was noisy and rattled about the motor because of Mr. Ezra's heavy foot and "no-caredness," as Mr. Nottoman described it.

Mr. Ezra brought the truck to an abrupt stop, honked the horn, and leaned over toward the right-hand window, which was partly covered with cardboard, replacing the broken glass. Melody could see the angry look on his face, which was not helped any by the wet brown snuff that drooled down each side of his mouth.

Mr. Nottoman and the other croppers, covered with tobacco gum, dirt, and sweat, moved toward the truck.

"Let me tell you one thing, John Nottoman," Mr. Ezra yelled without bothering to get out of the truck or to say good morning. "Somebody's been stealin' corn out of my corncrib, and I've a good notion that it's one of these helpers of yours, bein' as you got so cotton-pickin' many of 'em aroun' here!"

Jake gave a quick start toward the truck, his fists clenched. His son Isaac moved with him. Mr. Nottoman pulled his wet shirtsleeve. "Jake, you and Isaac go on and take out the mules. Buster will come and get you when we're ready to start work after dinner. It's just too hot to begin early."

Jake and Isaac moved away hesitantly.

Every muscle of Isaac's six-foot body was tense. His shoulders were broad and thick, his arms were long and muscular, and his hands were large enough to make another pair for an average man. In the summer he never wore shoes. In winter he cut big holes in the sides of each shoe to allow for the size of his foot. He seldom spoke unless he was angry, and he was seldom angry unless someone spoke of Mr. Ezra. When he became angry, big drops of sweat popped out of his forehead and blood-streaks lined his eyes. He didn't bother anyone, and he expected no one to bother him. He was the oldest son of Jake and Alice-Cora-Jane and was respected by his brothers and sisters equally with their father.

As he and Jake moved away, Isaac kept looking back to be sure that Mr. Ezra wasn't getting too close to Mr. Nottoman. He would have liked to hit Mr. Ezra a few seconds ago, right then and there, but Mr. Nottoman would not have allowed that. So he moved away silently and unwillingly. After all, to do what Mr. Nottoman said was the most important thing in the world to Isaac, even if it meant not hitting Mr. Ezra.

"Now see here, Ezra. Don't you come around here accusing my hands until you know what you're saying. You'd better consider getting a little proof before you accuse a man."

"I got proof. My corn's gone and that's all the proof I need. They'd just as soon steal as to live. I do hope I catch one of 'em."

"Now you just go on, Ezra, and try to find more pleasant business before you stop again," said Mr. Nottoman as he turned to walk away.

Mr. Ezra mashed the accelerator to the bottom. Blue puffs of smoke poured from beneath the motor's hood. The noise was so loud that Melody was forced to wait until he was around the bend before she spoke.

"Goodness, Papa. What's wrong with that man? Is he crazy or something? Jake wouldn't steal a toad-frog, or Isaac either. You know something, Papa. It wouldn't surprise me if Jake and Isaac don't beat him up one of these days."

"Melody, you're a girl and you shouldn't think about such things. Your mama needs you in the kitchen."

"You're right, Papa. But I can't help seeing and hearing, even if I can't understand. I'll be glad when my mind gets grown. Maybe I can understand folks like Mr. Ezra."

Mrs. Nottoman was warming dinner. It smelled so good that Melody thought she was going to faint from hunger before she could get the gum washed from her hands.

During the noon hour, the weatherman offered no hope of relief from the dry spell. But the tobacco was ripe and it had to be put in. About two-thirty Mr. Nottoman gave the work call, so Buster and Aaron caught the mules—Rodie and Kate—hitched them to the tobacco truck, put up the truck sheets, and drove to the field. The croppers' shirts were circled and stained with morning sweat. The noonday sun had dried them as they hung on the barnyard fence. The day dragged on. Pepsi-Cola time broke the long afternoon, as the mail had the morning. Five-cent cinnamon buns helped to fill the empty stomachs slightly nauseated by the smell of the sun-heated tobacco. By sunset enough sticks had been looped to fill the barn. The croppers came to the bench, went into the barn, and straddled the tier-poles that extended up and down and across the barn for hanging the tobacco. Melody, Martha, Mary, Jacob, Joseph, Aaron, and Abraham carried it to the barn door, where Mr. Nottoman or Buster took it and poked it to Isaac, the hanger on the bottom tier, or Jake, who hung

43

the top tiers. It was hot, and only Jacob and Joseph seemed to have enough energy left to scamper. They raced back to the racks, tried to "out-tote" each other, and skidded back and forth, in and out of the racks.

"It's all over for another day," sighed Melody when the last stick was in.

"For you but not for me," added her father.

"Oh, let me stay at the barn with you tonight, Papa. Please. I'll help you poke wood in the furnace and talk to you to keep you awake. Please, Papa-Daddy!"

"No teasing, Melody. I can hardly get you up in the morning when you sleep all night. If you stay awake, I'll never get you up."

"That's the solution to my problem. If I sit up all night, I won't have to get up in the morning! Please, Papa!"

"Melody," he replied, as they walked toward the house, "you don't make much sense for a twelve-year-old girl. You can't sit up all night."

"But next year, I'll be a teen-ager, Papa, and then I'll be smart enough to do lots of things. Why, you know, lots of girls get married when they're teen-agers. Late teen-agers, that is. You know something, Papa. Sometimes you—I mean life—just isn't fair. I help you cut bushes to put over the looping racks; I help you cut the weeds around the barn; I help you repair the furnace; I help you load sticks on the truck to haul to the barn;

44

I help you make truck sheets—and you won't even let me spend one little ol' night at the barn."

"That's a pretty good speech. How long did it take you to prepare it? Maybe you're in the wrong business. With your power of persuasion . . ."

"Oh, I can stay! I can stay! Buster, oh, Buster! When you cut the corn for the hogs, come back by the roasting ear patch and bring us a few young ears to roast in the furnace tonight. Eh, Papa? And bring a watermelon and a mushmelon, too!" yelled Melody.

"You know, it's a funny thing, Melody. You beg to stay up at the barn all night. Buster begs to stay at the house."

"It's a mixed-up world, Papa. A mixed-up world, but I love it—every minute of it—'specially since I can stay at the barn with you."

CHAPTER 5

IT WAS A BEAUTIFUL NIGHT. The stars were shining. The moon was coming up. There were fireflies everywhere. A pale, quick blink of lightning flickered in the north—a sign of fair weather, according to the old folks. Melody walked behind her father, carrying his lantern—for old times' sake—and her small, two-cell flashlight, a blanket, and a box of matches.

There was a sudden hum at Melody's ear.

"Uh, oh! Mosquitoes are out tonight. Wait, Papa, let me get an old guano bag to burn to smoke away the mosquitoes."

Mr. Nottoman stopped beside the fishpond to wait for Melody to get a tow bag from under the shelter. He flipped a match into the water, and a hungry little catfish was deceived and snapped at it. Small, lazy ripples took new positions in the pond. A water lily had covered its face for the night. The air was stifling—there was no rain in sight.

"You know something, Papa. Buster is a real peculiar. Anybody who doesn't like to sleep at a tobacco barn is a real puzzle. It must be downright painful to grow up and have to go courting and dress up and put on sweet-smelling stuff like Buster does."

"Let's not talk about Buster when he isn't here to defend himself."

"Oh, I meant no harm, Papa. But I just can't understand his not wanting to stay at the barn."

The wood had almost burned away in the log barn. Mr. Nottoman added a few pieces of dried gum wood. It took only a little heat for the yellowing stage. At the next barn the kerosene stoker gave a slight hum and then a loud blow. "Well, at least that's working all right," Mr. Nottoman said, relieved.

"Papa, I don't see why we don't put coal stokers or kerosene stokers in all the barns. It would be a lot less trouble and . . ." Melody clasped her hands quickly over her mouth.

"And we wouldn't have to sit up at the barn at night," added her father.

"I'm sorry, Papa. I really am. I like the little ol' wood-eating log barn. It cures the prettiest tobacco every time and the tobacco smells so good—just like real tobacco should. You said yourself that tobacco cured with oil and coal was just as different from wood-cured tobacco as pit-cooked barbecue was different from oven-cooked meat."

"You never forget a thing, do you, Melody?"

"Well, I don't know. Anyway, I don't see any need of forgetting something you know just to keep from remembering. It's all right if I remember all I hear if I want to, eh, Papa?"

Melody took a small twig from the woodpile, held it in the furnace, waited till it was burning, and then stuck it against the guano bag until the bag was aflame. She fanned the bag in the breeze until it was burning well and then swung it in the darkness. It made a circle of fire against the night. Then she laid it on the ground, folded it in itself, and smothered it so that it gave off only a slight smoke, sending forth a fertilizery odor into the thick night air.

"No mosquitoes tonight. They can't stand our smoky perfume. Right, Papa?"

Melody was preparing her bed for the night. She put up each side of the tobacco truck and then hung truck sheets on all sides. She folded the other truck sheets for a pillow and a mattress. "Hope all the tobacco fleas have gone back to the tobacco patch," she said as she crawled in, not really intending to go to sleep.

No breeze was stirring. Only the occasional call of a cricket to his mate or a rainfrog begging for a refreshing bath broke the stillness. The crackling wood in the furnace sent sparks from its burning mouth. Familiar sounds. Expected sounds. Peaceful sounds.

48

"Footsteps?" said Melody to herself. She peeked over the curtain hesitantly, expectantly. A stooped shadow crept down the path toward them, a mass of blackness in the moonlight.

"Papa, Papa. Look!" said Melody softly. "It's Mr. Ezra. Look, Papa. What on earth does he want?"

"Lie down, Melody, and keep quiet. Or maybe you'd better go to the house."

"If it's all right with you, I'll lie down and be quiet and I won't even listen. Really, I'll try not to."

Mr. Ezra came nearer—brown, weather-beaten, tall, thin as a stalk of corn and weighing about as much. He had deep-set blue eyes, big ears, and little broken bluish-red blood vessels in his protruding cheekbones— vessels popped by too much stump-hole liquor, his tenants said. As he approached Mr. Nottoman, he kept clearing his throat as if he had something important to say.

"Nottoman, I'm here on important business and I don't have but a minute, so I'll come right to the point. I want to know didn't you have no more sense than to take that young'un of Jake's to a white folks' hospital. And as if that wasn't enough, you gave your consent for him and his mama to spend the night there! I bet if the neighbors knew, you wouldn't be as important around here as you think you are."

"I guess the neighbors know. It's no secret. In fact,

some of them gave blood for transfusions this morning."

"Don't you give me no sass talk. I just wanted you to know that I think you're just about the most brazen piece of man I've seen in many a day taking that young'un to the same hospital that I go to."

"Look, Ezra. You're in no shape to reason with. That child was bleeding to death and had had a hard knock on the head. It was a matter of life and death, and when it comes to life and death, life and death are all that matter."

"What if he had of died? What difference would it of made?"

"Now I tell you what, Ezra. You just go on back home and sleep this off. You'll get over it in a few days!"

"Don't you preach to me. First thing you know, they'll want to be marrying up with the white folks, and that will be the last of the pure white strain like Ezra Bowles. And you'd better watch out. Your little upstart of a daughter might be the first one to marry a . . ."

Mr. Nottoman jumped up quickly. He reached for a tobacco stick that was sitting against the barn. Melody raised up quickly. Mr. Ezra moved back—three or four steps.

"Ezra, you get away from here, right now. I mean right now!"

Mr. Nottoman's voice was quivering. In the firelight Melody could see her father as he stiffened, gritted his teeth, and stuck the stick at least a foot into the soft ground.

"See what I told you," said Mr. Ezra, as he backed away. "Just look at her—sleeping at a tobacco barn. You're all mixed up about raising young'uns—Melody at the barn and Buster at the house. You're one mixed-up man."

By that time, Melody was standing beside her father. Mr. Ezra continued to back away, mumbling to himself as he hastened his steps and moved out of sight.

Everything was silent for a moment except for the crackling fire. A whippoorwill awoke and complained about the noise.

"Goodness, Papa. What's the matter with Mr. Ezra? Is he crazy or something? Goodness, if I hated anything as bad as he hates Jake's family, I think my heart would split wide open. And what did he mean about me sleeping at the barn? He sure is mixed up about good things in life, isn't he, Papa?"

Mr. Nottoman sat there for a minute and then said, "Well, you see, Melody, some people just get all warped and twisted and mixed-up. They don't even know why themselves. And when they get older, they're ashamed to change, and they just go on and on without knowing where or why." Mr. Nottoman paused for a moment. "We're both tired and it's been a long hard day. We must try to get some rest."

CHAPTER 6

"Look, Papa! Look!" Melody yelled early the next morning. "There's smoke coming from over beyond Mr. Ezra's. Something's on fire!"

"My goodness! There sure is. Let's hope it's not a home or a packhouse, Melody. A tobacco barn would be bad enough."

Mr. Nottoman called to Mrs. Nottoman that he and Melody were going to the fire.

"Whose place is it, John?"

"Looks like Mr. Lloyd's, but I'm not sure."

"Buster ought to go," said Mr. Nottoman as he and Melody got into the truck. "He could help tote water, but we can't wait for him to get up. He's more of a sleepyhead than you sometimes."

"Look, Papa. The smoke is turning red. The flames are really leaping up. Can't you make old Betsy go faster?"

"Melody, this truck won't . . ."

"I know, Papa. I'm sorry. You don't have to explain."

It was Mr. Lloyd's tobacco barn. When he had left the barn to go to eat breakfast, according to a neighbor who talked to Melody, a stick had fallen on the flue, and before anyone knew it, the whole barn was on fire and five hundred sticks of tobacco were in flames.

"It seems hopeless," said Melody as she joined the line of neighbors—black, white, young, old—passing buckets of water, hand to hand, from the Lloyds' well. Another crew brought buckets- and bucketsful from the neighbor's house across the way. But the flames were so hot and leaped so high that no one could really get close enough to throw on enough water to kill the blaze.

On the porch stood Mr. Lloyd's wife and five small children. They were too terrified to move.

Finally, there was a great crash. The barn had fallen in. The bucket brigade moved back. It was all over except the final moments of burning. They had done all they could, but it had not been enough.

Melody felt a tear trickle down her cheek.

Mr. Nottoman stood with a group of men, their faces red and their brows and shirts sweat-drenched.

After a few moments the crowd moved away—slowly, hesitantly. It was a grim reminder that any one of them could be next. Tobacco season took its toll of several barns in every community. The danger was not over until the last ember had died and the last stoker switch had been pushed.

After asking a neighbor, who had started toward Mr. Nottoman, to tell her father that she was going to walk home, Melody wandered off by herself, not wanting anyone, especially her father, to see her tears. She was, after all, almost a teen-ager now, and she should start acting like one. Before she realized it, she was nearly home. The brown dirt on the side of the asphalt highway was warm under her feet. It felt good, and she could not help thinking of the peace and quiet of the morning while she and her father were at the tobacco barn. Then, suddenly, the fire had started. Why did there have to be bad things like fires? It was hard for her to understand these things that always seemed to happen just when life was so quiet and enjoyable.

Small beads of sweat from the heat of the burning barn and her exertion in the bucket brigade still covered Melody's forehead. She wiped them with the sleeve of her blouse. It smelled like wood smoke. She started to turn down the little road, but she saw a strange greenish-brown pickup truck parked beside the highway a short distance from where she had stopped. Two men in tan uniforms were measuring spaces with a tape and setting up little white posts, three of which she could see from where she stood.

"Airport men, I just know they are," Melody mumbled. "Wonder if Papa and Mama have noticed them. I wish they'd go away and never come back—to measure for an airport anyway."

Her first reaction would have been to run for the

house, but one of the uniformed men saw her and waved. She waved back halfheartedly and walked slowly towards where the men were working. The man who had waved was tall and thin. His face was narrow and brown from the sun, and his sandy hair was peppered with gray like her father's. The other man was short and stocky, with a round red face and sharp blue eyes.

"Good morning, young lady," the tall man said, as his companion nodded hurriedly and then continued to write on a piece of paper attached to a clipboard.

"Good morning, gentlemen." Melody smiled a little, hesitated, and then asked, "Are you men here surveying for the airport project?"

"Why, yes, we are," the friendly one answered, "but how would a young lady like you know about such projects?"

"Well," Melody replied, "I live in that house across the road—Big Oaks, we call it—and I'm mighty worried about where the airport is going to be."

"I can understand that, young lady," the surveyor said, nodding his head in emphasis, "but I'm afraid there's a very good chance that this is where it will be."

"I was afraid of that when I saw you here," Melody answered. Her voice was beginning to choke. "But thank you for letting me know."

"You're welcome. And don't you worry too much,"

the surveyor added. "Things usually work out for the best."

"Yes, sir. I'll try not to."

The other surveyor was in the truck, fumbling with a set of papers that lay on the front seat. Melody knew that he would not see her if she waved good-bye, and she really didn't want to wave good-bye to him anyway. "He doesn't care," thought Melody, as the tears and anger swelled within her. "He doesn't care about Big Oaks or me or anything but the airport.

"Somebody's got to find a way to save Big Oaks; somebody's got to!" she kept saying over and over as she clenched her fists and hastened her steps, making her dark hair fly in the wind. She swallowed hard—a choking swallow. The wind felt good against her face. She could see Mama now, standing at the back door, waiting to hear about the fire and maybe about the surveyors. She would tell Mama everything she had heard, but there was a part she couldn't tell. It had something to do with what Papa called "every man bearing his own burden"—and she was still working on that part.

CHAPTER 7

IT WAS ONE OF THOSE DAYS in late July when it was 93 degrees in the shade, even before noon. But Mr. Nottoman was worried about the small, green suckers now growing between the leaves. So he and Buster and Melody, with Jake's family, spent the entire day breaking the suckers from the stalks.

That night Melody went to bed early, only to be awakened around midnight by a loud crack of thunder and a bright flash of lightning. When she tried to turn on the light in her room, there was no electricity. Outside, the oaks were hissing and rustling in the strong wind. Her mother had not wakened her and apparently had hoped that she would sleep through the storm.

Fumbling cautiously, she made her way toward the living room. Mrs. Nottoman met her, carrying a candle.

"Sure is a bad storm, isn't it, Mama?"

"Yes. You come stay with us until it's over," answered Mrs. Nottoman.

Mr. Nottoman, Buster, and Teddy were all in the living room.

Outside, the wind continued to roar about the house and through the oaks. Thunder rumbled. Quick, blue streaks seemed to walk right through the windowpane. Suddenly there was a crash, seemingly loud enough to burst the eardrums.

"That sure struck nearby," said Mr. Nottoman, announcing a fact already evident to the tense family.

Wind roared and thunder rumbled.

"Wind, wind, wind," sighed Melody.

"Don't complain, Melody," corrected Mrs. Nottoman.

"I'm sorry. I didn't mean to, Mama."

Heavy drops of rain beat against the windowpane and on the tin roof.

"Hail, Papa?" questioned Melody, her heart pounding heavily from anxiety.

"Those sounds are a bit heavy for rain. But we'll see. We can't be sure yet."

"Storms in the daytime are bad, but storms at night are worse. Papa, you reckon this is blowing down the tobacco and tearing it to shreds?" continued Melody.

"Maybe not. We'll see."

Another hard, sudden crash announced that lightning had struck nearby again.

"This is a typical, summer storm. There very seldom comes a bad storm that lightning doesn't strike one of the oaks in the yard," said Mr. Nottoman.

"Let's cut them down, Papa."

"Melody!"

"Well, Papa, that's the only solution I know," defended Melody.

"But you can't run from God. So far, it's never struck the house, and that's a blessing! Think of all the cool shade the trees give."

"I didn't mean any harm, Papa. I'm just scared, I guess."

After about twenty minutes, the storm suddenly seemed to fade away like a fast-moving freight train.

"Quietness after a storm is like returning to a house after a burying," commented Mrs. Nottoman.

"Can we go out, Papa? We can use the flashlight. Maybe we can see the tobacco."

"Not yet, Melody. Sometimes the most dangerous lightning follows the storm just as the calm begins. We'd better wait a minute."

"I'll get my raincoat and overshoes if I can borrow a candle," said Melody, as she and her mother got up to leave.

"You know, Mama, I'm sorry I said ugly things about getting up early to work in the tobacco."

Mrs. Nottoman didn't comment.

Outside, broken limbs and twigs and leaves were scattered over the yard. Mr. Nottoman flashed the light toward the cornfield. It seemed a twisted mess. He moved the flashlight hesitantly toward the tobacco patch. Melody partially covered her eyes with her hands and breathed deeply.

"Lordy, Papa. It's blown down, too." Melody ran ahead of him in the path of light.

"Come back, Melody. We've had a bad hail and wind storm, but you can't tell much about it tonight."

"But the Lord will think we don't care."

"Oh, Melody. It's the heart that counts at times like these, not actions."

Together they approached the tobacco field. Melody watched the white beam from her father's flashlight play fitfully over the fallen stalks. But she could not satisfy herself. Try as she might, she could not see far into the patch through the blackness.

Weariness beckoned her to bed; but, for a long time, she tossed and tumbled, unable to sleep. Finally, she got out of bed and lowered her window. The breeze after the hailstorm was too cool for comfort.

"I'll never complain again about getting up," she prayed. "I'll never fuss about the resetting and chopping and worming and suckering and topping or anything. And I'll even marry a farmer if I love him, and he loves me. Honest, God. Don't let Papa's tobacco all be destroyed. I'll be a better girl when I get to be a teenager and my mind grows up."

Melody knew there would be money for school clothes and school lunches. Papa would find a way to provide, even if they had to borrow money from the borrowed money. But that did not help Teddy's fund—not at all. If the crop was destroyed, that would be all for another year. Another Thanksgiving, another Christmas, another Easter, another spring, another planting season—all of these—even another school year, before another crop could be grown and sold. In the meantime, there could be no doctor for Teddy.

CHAPTER 8

AWAKENED THE NEXT MORNING by the sound of Jake's and Mr. Nottoman's voices, Melody jumped out of bed, ran to the window, raised the shade, and looked at the tobacco. It was a shocking sight. Twisted, over-turned stalks, ragged leaves! Not even a visible row space in sight. Even the truck rows were covered with tobacco. Grabbing her dungarees, sweat shirt, and ten-nis shoes, she dressed as quickly as possible and ran to the tobacco patch.

"Do you think we can save it, Papa?" she asked in a choked voice.

"Well, yes and no. The damage is severe, but we can still save a little of it, we hope. It may not sell as good and be as pretty, but anyway, even if we don't have the best, we have something. The neighbors were hit hard too."

"What about Mr. Ezra, Papa? Was he hit hard?"

"Harder than we were," he replied.

After breakfast Jake and Mary and Martha and Abra-ham, with Buster, Melody, and Mr. Nottoman, set up the leaning stalks of tobacco by lifting them, setting them straight, and pushing dirt against them with their feet. Broken leaves were placed in the tobacco truck whether the leaves were ripe or not.

"De Lawd done whupped us sho' 'nough last night, ain't He, Mr. Nottoman?" asked Jake, as they rested at the end of the rows and surveyed the hopelessness behind and ahead.

"Well, we can't exactly call it a whipping, Jake. Maybe it's just a reminder that there's a Higher Power than we are and that man doesn't control and own anything really. You see, Jake, the Lord moves in mysterious ways, His wonders to perform."

"Mr. Nottoman, you got mo' faith dan a preacher an' you sounds jist like one, 'specially in times o' trouble. You ain't right sure you ain't missed yore callin', is you?"

"We've got to be thankful, Jake, that the storm wasn't any worse or more widespread. At least we had only two croppings left. Most of our tobacco is already safely packed in the barn."

"Now don't git me wrong, Mr. Nottoman. I don't doubt Gawd an' I ain't lost faith. I jist likes to hear you 'splain things in a Bible way."

The crew started on a new set of rows. The work was slow and tedious. Leaves on the ground had to be picked up before the workers or the mules and truck could move ahead to set up the leaning stalks. The day was bright, but thick-hot, heavy-hot. The broiling sun drew from the earth enough moisture to sicken the air. Sweat poured from the foreheads of the workers. Dark, wet, extended circles were under every arm of every shirt unless the whole shirt was saturated with perspiration.

Mr. Nottoman, Jake, Isaac, and Buster moved up their rows, somewhat more rapidly than the younger workers. Realizing that the children were far behind him, Isaac was eager to talk about Mr. Ezra.

"You know, Mr. Nottoman, life ain't really so bad, an' it's purty nigh easy to fin' somethin' good in everythin' 'ceptin' dat Mr. Ezra."

"Now don't get him on your mind again, Isaac. Mr. Ezra has plenty of trouble with this hail without having you for an enemy."

"But I jist don't like dat man. I swear I don't!"

Jake stood upright. "What you say, boy! I'll git one o' dese hail-beat-up stalks an' whup you good if you swears like dat."

"Yas, suh. But I jist don't like dat man. He called all o' us thiefs an' I jist ain't fo' sho' gonna have nobody callin' me an' my folkses thiefs."

"Oh, Isaac, you just forget about Ezra and the thief accusation. He was just trying to stir up a little excitement. You know how it is during tobacco season. Everybody gets tired and worried and ill and nobody acts like himself," said Mr. Nottoman.

64

"I know, Mr. Nottoman, but dat man mus' raise 'baccer all year roun', 'cause he stays ill an' worried all de time. You know somethin'? I ain't never, I mean *never* seen him smile. An' you know what else, Mr. Nottoman? Dey say dat man takes his lantern an' goes out to dat ol' crib barn ever' night an' watches to see if he can see who's stealin' his corn. An' you know somethin' else, Mr. Nottoman? I bet he ain't missed no corn nohow. De warf rats, dey coulda carried off a ear or two, but Mr. Ezra, he couldn't never miss dat."

"I don't know," spoke up Jake before he thought. "Dat Mr. Ezra sho' is a stingy man. I bet he's got mo' dollars hid in shoe boxes an' fruit jars an' trunks dan any o' us has ever seen. He sho' ain't never spent none, an' I knows he ain't never give none away. I bet if it costed anythin', dat man wouldn't even breathe."

"Jake," reprimanded Mr. Nottoman, "you're too much of a man to be ruined by hatred for Mr. Ezra, and besides, you mustn't talk that way around your children. They learn to think and act just like you do, you know."

"I knows dat Miss Melody jist like you, Mr. Nottoman, but I doubts my chillen is jist like me," answered Jake, seeming rather embarrassed at his sudden outburst.

"But, Jake, they learn to think like the older people

they live with, and thinking is powerful stuff. In fact, it's the thing that makes us what we are," explained Mr. Nottoman.

"Oh, you mean we ain't dust an' clay an' spittle like de Good Book says, Mr. Nottoman?"

"Yes, we're dust and clay and spittle perhaps, but we're more than that, Jake. We're mind and conscience and soul and lots of other things too."

"I guess I sees what you means now."

Meanwhile, Melody called a brief, excited conference with the younger workers.

"Hey, all of you. I know a secret. A big, good one. If we work hard and finish early enough, I'll get a dozen eggs from Mama to trade at the store for candy. She's already promised them."

"But we'll have to go by Mr. Ezra's. Dat kinda stops my wants fo' candy," said Abraham.

"Oh, Abraham. We'd put a bag over your face and lead you through the fire, like they do a mule, if you were really scared, but you're not scared."

"Yes, I is. I sho' 'nough is."

"We'll look after you. I promise," said Melody.

With renewed enthusiasm, the little crew returned to work.

"Slow work, isn't it, Papa?" said Melody, when she and the other young hands caught up.

"Yes, slow and tedious. Sometimes I wonder if it's

worth trying to save. These leaves are so beaten and broken and almost none are ripe. But I reckon we'd better try to save them. Maybe we can sell them for scrap or something."

"Scrap or something." That meant no tips. The tobacco already harvested couldn't begin to sell for enough to pay the debts on the crop. Melody worked on, thinking over and over again about the dream, the hope, the sugar bag.

CHAPTER 9

ABOUT MIDAFTERNOON, when the field work was finished, Melody and the six Binger children made their way toward the country store. Aaron whistled. Martha tried to see how far she could kick the sand. Melody suggested that they play follow the leader, and they did. An abandoned farmhouse that had the reputation of being haunted caused them to walk faster. As they approached Mr. Ezra's house, each one paused, almost unconsciously.

"There's no one at home at Mr. Ezra's. Come on, everybody. Even if he is there, he's not going to bother us," coaxed Melody.

"Don't say dat, Miss Melody. Dat man is bad. Jist look at his house. It looks like a ghostes' place."

"Oh, Abraham. Come on. You don't believe in ghosts any more than I do," teased Melody.

"I believes in bad folkses, an' I sho' is skeered to go by Mr. Ezra's, even if he ain't dere."

"My goodness, Abraham. We've got more important things to worry about. We've got to decide what kind of candy we're going to buy."

"Let's buy Mary Janes. Dey's three o' dem to a pack," suggested Mary.

"O.K. All for Mary Janes raise your hands," said Melody.

The vote was unanimous.

At the store, Mr. Dodd, a short, fat man with a tiny red face, explained that eggs were forty cents a dozen. That meant forty blocks of candy, three pieces to each block.

"All Mary Janes, please," said Melody.

"All Mary Janes? Are you sure?"

"Yes, we voted unanimous. Every one of us."

Mr. Dodd dropped forty Mary Janes into a paper bag. Joseph grinned.

"Thank you, Mr. Dodd. Thank you very much," said the group together as they left.

Outside, they sat down beside the road in a grassy spot and distributed the candy, one package at a time. They each had five blocks. "What shall we do with the five extra ones?" asked Melody, puzzled.

"Take dem to yore Mama, Melody. Bet she loves Mary Janes, too."

"Oh, Mama doesn't really like candy. She's afraid she'll get fat, I guess."

"I sho' likes Mary Janes," said Mary, as she hopped twice and skipped three times, making it a sort of rhythmic game but trying especially to show the red ruffles of the fluff petticoat that Melody had outgrown and given to her.

"You jist like me. You likes Mary Janes 'cause dey so good," said Aaron.

"Wrong. Dead wrong."

"You likes Mary Janes 'cause dey's wrapped in purty yellow paper to match yore yellow ribbon," guessed Martha.

"Wrong. Dead wrong."

"We give up. You'll have to tell us," coaxed Melody.

"I likes Mary Janes 'cause dey's got part o' my name."

"Who on earth woulda' ever noticed dat? You sho' is a braggin' girl. You ain't got no right to claim no part o' de namin' o' dis candy!" said Abraham.

"All right. Y'all better not fuss. I'll tell Mama Alice-Cora-Jane an' she'll whup all o' us good 'nough. You knows what she tol' us. She ain't gonna have no Cains an' Abels in dis here family," warned Martha.

"You know what, Miss Melody? Dey's some bad folkses in de Bible like Cain an' Abel an' Jezebel. You ever read 'bout Jezebel?"

She slapped her hand over her mouth. "Lawd, what is I done said?"

"You done tol' family secret stuff. Mama Alice-Cora-Jane done tol' you not to say nothin' 'bout what we says 'bout Jezebel. I'm sho' gonna tell Mama Alice-Cora-Jane," threatened Mary.

"Please. Please don't. A piece o' Mary Jane not to tell," Martha pleaded.

"A good bargain-swap. Hand it over," demanded Mary.

"It ain't fair an' it ain't a even swap, but I done said what I done said an' I guess I's jist got to pay fo' it," complained Martha.

"Pay me or Mama Alice-Cora-Jane," threatened Mary.

Martha grudgingly handed Mary a piece of her candy.

Thick woods lined both sides of the road. Pines, oaks, maples, and sycamores cast long, cool shadows across the road. Jacob came from behind the group.

"Y'all know somethin'! I's been walkin' behin' y'all ever since we left dat sto' and I's been countin' Mary Jane papers. Some o' us is eatin' too slow, an' some o' us is eatin' too fast. We ain't all eatin' jist alike. Some o' us's candy is gonna' be all gone an' some o' us is gonna have a heap o' candy left, an' dat ain't right. Dat ain't no way fo' friends to do."

"Oh, Jacob. You're not being fair. Everybody was given five blocks of candy with three pieces each. Everyone has the right to eat it as he wishes," defended Melody.

"But Miss Melody. Supposin' we gits to workin' to-morrow an' everybody has some candy but me. Dat sho' is gonna make me awful powerful hungry," murmured Jacob. "Let's make everybody sit down an' show his candy, an' den we can all eat a piece at de same time an' all de candy'll be gone at de same time!" he suggested.

"You'll never get approval of that," said Melody.

"If it'll make him happy, why not, Miss Melody? He ain't gonna git none o' nobody's nohow. An' I got secret places to hide a piece if I wants to save a piece; ain't you, Miss Melody?" asked Martha.

"Oh, I doubt that, and we'll have no cheating like hiding candy," said Melody. "Everyone who is in favor of counting candy, sit down over here on the edge of the road in the shade," suggested Melody.

"Why not? I's dead tired anyway. I sho' is," added Mary.

"All right. No cheating now. No hiding candy. Everybody put all the candy he has left in his hand or lap or somewhere where it can be seen," commanded Melody. She began to count. "Eighteen blocks left out of thirty-five," she announced finally.

"Nope. Dat ain't right. I ain't found dat many pieces o' Mary Jane papers. Somebody's lyin', 'cause if somebody didn't have some hid candy, I'd have mo' pieces o' paper. Right?"

"Oh, Jacob. You're really being unreasonable. Come on, everybody. Let me count one more time," suggested Melody, a bit disgusted.

"Eighteen pieces is right," announced Melody. "Maybe you didn't find all the pieces of paper. Maybe one blew away."

"No, ma'am. I was watchin' close. Somebody's hidin' candy."

"Anybody hiding candy?" questioned Melody.

Nobody spoke. "O.K. In the beginning this was just a joke because everybody's candy was his own business. But now it's a question of honesty. And that means that we're concerned about right and wrong. Anybody got anything to say?" questioned Melody.

Everyone was silent. A rabbit jumped from the bushes, saw the little gang, and turned and hopped quickly into the woods again. A blue jay squawked.

"You all know something? In just a little while we'll be at the old house, and if there's anyone in this group who's not being completely honest about his candy, that person might be just the one that old ghost comes out to haunt," warned Melody.

Everybody looked at everybody else. "Lawd, Miss Melody. Don't talk like dat. Ghostes is de worstest subject in de whole United States world," said Mary, trembling.

"Well, we've got to be sure everybody's honest. The devil is worse than the ghosts," warned Melody.

"Miss Melody, I hates to correct you, but you ain't supposed to say 'devil.' Mama Alice-Cora-Jane said

73

dat am a sinful word. De word to use am 'bad man,' "
said Martha hesitantly, but knowingly.

"O.K., Martha. I was wrong. You are right. 'Devil'
is a bad word, 'specially when there's a good substitute
with the same meaning."

Abraham stood up. There was fear in his eyes. "I have
a 'fession to make, Miss Melody. When I et my candy, I
et de paper too. You sees, some o' de Mary Jane sticks to
de paper, an' I jist couldn't bear to throw none o' de
candy away."

"Me, too," confessed Joseph. "I et my paper, too."

Melody laughed. "You see, if everybody's honest, we
have no problem."

"Oh, yes we do," said Aaron. "We still got five blocks
o' candy left. Who gits 'em?"

"Melody's Mama," said Martha, proud that she was
smart enough to remember the original suggestion.

"Mama doesn't like candy much. Maybe we could
think of something else. Let's all think a minute."

Melody, in deep thought, propped her elbows on her
knees and lowered her face into her open, uplifted
palms. The others did likewise, as if they, too, were
thinking. Suddenly Melody spoke. "You all know something? We're the most selfish bunch in the whole world.
We've been to the store and eaten candy and had a big
time, and we've not even thought of Little Moses and

Teddy. The extra five pieces go to them. All in favor, stand up!"

All arose, and the smiles showed unanimous approval of Melody's suggestion. "Any more problems?" questioned Melody.

Jacob bowed his head. "Miss Melody, I's caused enough trouble. I's not gonna say nothin' else 'bout eatin' candy or savin' candy, but I sho' wish you'd tell everybody not to save a whole lot of his'n till mine's gone. When I gits hungry fo' candy, I gits powerful hungry."

"You've already stated your problem and your wishes," comforted Melody. "And you're among friends. I doubt that anybody has enough willpower to save a piece of Mary Jane even until we get back home."

As they stood up to continue toward home, Abraham yelled excitedly, "Look, look, Miss Melody. Yonder comes Mr. Ezra on his truck. What in de worl' is we gonna do?"

"Nothing, Abraham. Just act natural. He's not going to bother us."

"But he might. Let's hide in de woods!"

The others voted for this idea by their actions and expressions.

"No, no. Mr. Ezra won't bother us if we don't bother him."

By this time, Mr. Ezra had almost reached them. He slowed down as if he were going to stop, but suddenly mashed the accelerator as if he couldn't get away fast enough. The frightened children watched him as he drove by his own house.

"You know what, Miss Melody. Dey sez dat poison dirt grows poison weeds on his farm. If you walk on his land, you'll die in a minute."

"Oh, no, Joseph. That couldn't possibly be true."

"I bet it is. I jist bet."

"We'll see. We'll just stop by there on our way back."

"You'll never git me to stop. I's skeered, an' besides, Mama Alice-Cora-Jane would wear us out. She tol' us not to never bother Mr. Ezra. She sho' 'nough did," added Mary.

But when they got to Mr. Ezra's, Melody turned toward the barn that stood beside the road.

"No, Miss Melody. Don't go dat way. Please. We's skeered o' poisoned weeds an' poisoned dirt."

"No, I'm not going to work and play with friends that believe such nonsense. Come on!"

Hesitantly, the others followed, each from time to time looking in every direction to be sure that Mr. Ezra did not suddenly reappear.

"See, we're not dying. Not a one of us!"

By this time, they were behind the barn.

"Look at dat ragged ol' hole in de barn, Miss Melody.

I bet dat's where Mr. Ezra sneaks in to guard his corn so nobody won't see him go in de front door an' know he's dere."

"What an imagination, Abraham. The hole is too little for anybody to go through. You know that."

"All I knows is I wants to git away from dis hole, dis barn, an' dis place afore Mr. Ezra turns aroun' an' comes back here an' gits us," said Abraham, hastening his steps.

It was almost sunset when the happy, but exhausted, group got back to Big Oaks. After the other children had left, Melody picked up a copy of the Wilson paper. When she looked at the headlines, she ran to Mr. Nottoman, who was standing near the packhouse. "Oh, look, Papa, this paper tells about the opening of the tobacco markets in Wilson Thursday week. Please let me go to the opening!"

"Melody, don't get carried away. It's too early to plan yet. Too much work to do. Lugs to grade and tie up for market and everything."

"I'll declare, Papa. Work! Work! And school starts the next week, and then it will be work, work, work, work. . . ."

"Melody, don't exaggerate."

"I'm not, Papa. Really, though."

"Oh, we shall see. We might get to the opening, but it means a lot of work, work, work!"

After the routine of a day's barning, Melody helped her father load lugs from the packhouse onto the truck to take them to the racks so the dampness of the night would make them soft and flexible and they could be taken off the sticks and tied in bundles.

"Reckon they'll weigh two pounds a stick, Papa?"

"Might."

"Two pounds at fifty cents a pound. A dollar a stick!"

"Don't assume too much before the market opens. We need more than fifty cents a pound."

"This has been an expensive crop, hasn't it, Papa?"

"Oh, yes, as always."

"Papa," said Melody after she had been silent a moment, "I hope I didn't see a secret, but awhile ago, I saw a little ol' pile of green oak wood lying beside the barn. And last year when I found a little ol' pile of oak wood in almost the same place, it wasn't many days before I smelled a little ol' barbecue pig cooking."

Mr. Nottoman smiled. "Well, well. You think you've seen a secret and you've almost made a riddle of it. Now why didn't you just come right out and ask me in plain language, 'Papa, are we going to have a barbecue at the end of this putting-in season?' "

"Psychology, Papa. Using psychology—like you use on Mama when you really want her to do something!"

"Melody, where on earth did you learn that word?"

"Oh, I listen and I observe. I've heard you say the

word many a time, and I've seen it in action more than that. We are going to have a barbecue, aren't we, Papa? I hate for that little ol' red pig to have to die, but I can just smell it already, and my mouth is already watering. Huh! Good ol' salty brown skin sizzling over the hot coals; salty, browned spareribs flavored with vinegar and hot pepper. Gosh, Papa. Let's cook it right now. I'm starving already."

"Don't dream too fast, Melody. We can't take off time to cook a barbecue just yet. Little grading still to do."

"But we *are* going to have one, aren't we, Papa? I know we are. Oh, boy! Baked sweet potatoes, good ol' oven-cooked corn bread, cole slaw, Brunswick stew, boiled potatoes with tomato sauce, and plenty of Pepsis and watermelon and everything—right here under this shelter with Alice-Cora-Jane and her whole family. Papa, I can just see Little Moses now, with a big sparerib in one hand and a piece of corn bread in the other, trying to decide which to eat first!"

"Melody, you are a dreamer. But we'll see about the barbecue after the lugs are graded."

CHAPTER 10

IT WAS LATE AUGUST. The days seemed a little hazy, and the nights were longer. Though the days were still hot, the nights were cooler. Especially in the early morning, the aroma of tobacco filled the air.

On the Saturday morning prior to the opening of the tobacco market, the airport hearing was held. Mr. Nottoman asked Melody if she would like to go with him to the Wilson courtroom. He knew how interested she was in the proceedings, and he told her she could sit in the back and just listen.

Melody and Mr. Nottoman were among the first to arrive. Melody watched her father as he walked toward the front of the room. She noticed that the walls were pale green and were smudged with fingerprints and grease spots that hinted of crowded courtroom days when spectators had leaned against them. Large portraits of serious-looking men in black robes looked down on the courtroom, giving it an appearance of dignity and mystery, Melody thought. Wine-colored velvet curtains, faded from the sun, were drawn back to the edges of the opened windows, and Venetian blinds, gray with age, were raised as high as they could be pulled. The heat from the morning sun poured into the musty-smelling room, though occasionally a hint of a breeze stirred the curtains.

This courtroom is hotter than the middle of a tobacco patch at noon, Melody thought, as she wiped sweat from her forehead with her hands. She strained her eyes to see the front of the room, but even with the sunlight the room was gloomy and half-dark. Two small electric lamps lit up the platform in front just enough that Melody could see the people sitting there. But she could not be seen.

The man who did most of the talking was lean and tall. His hair was dark and a little shaggy. He wore a black suit and black tie and sat on the left side of the little platform. The seven farmers, including Mr. Nottoman, sat opposite him on the right.

Melody thought that her father looked especially handsome in his white shirt, dark tie, and gray trousers. She could not see his shoes, but she knew they were all right. She had polished them yesterday after the yard was swept, and Teddy had rubbed them with an old work sock this morning to give an extra shine.

"Gentlemen," the man in the black suit began, "I want you to know at the start that nothing definite has been decided about the location of the airport."

Mr. Nottoman and the six other farmers looked very serious as the man explained the need for an airport in the region and tried to get them to see that their land was a good location and that an airport there would benefit the whole community.

None of the farmers seemed to agree with him. Melody could tell by the expressions on their faces.

Mr. Nottoman was chairman of the group, and after the man in the black suit had finished, he spoke in a calm, clear voice. He explained that the seven represented about 150 people who had attended a community meeting a few nights before and that they had a petition signed by all these people to present to him.

"We do not appeal in anger or with any ill will," Mr. Nottoman continued. "We realize that our area is a good, central location for an airport, but we believe our farms could do more to help mankind as they are. We're selfish, in a human way. We don't want to lose our farms. But we also sincerely believe that maybe you and your commission could find some land somewhere that is not so good for farming. The names on this petition represent people who all have the same feeling.

He handed the petition to the man in the black coat.

The man's face remained expressionless as he glanced quickly at the petition.

Melody's heart began to beat faster. In fact, she thought it was going to "bust clean out" of her chest. Her face flushed. They seemed to be getting nowhere with the man in the black suit. She must say something. But she hadn't asked Papa if it would be all right for her to speak. She tried to calm herself. Her hands began to sweat. Maybe she was going to faint, or have a heart attack or something.

She had to speak. That was all there was to it! She just had to. She arose, went down the aisle, stood before the man in the black suit, and waited to be recognized. She dared not look at Papa and the six other farmers.

The man nodded to her and smiled. He looked much younger close up, she mused.

"Please do not think I'm trying to be smart," Melody began. "I realize I'm young and can't think like grown folks. But I do have a heart and feelings. I'm old enough to know how it's going to feel to have to give up our home and farm and neighbors and move away."

The man nodded in understanding, as the tall surveyor had done that day after Mr. Lloyd's fire. This man is no monster, Melody thought as she caught her breath. He wants to understand, too.

"We know," she continued, "that the airport has to be built somewhere, but can't you and your men find some woods or some wasteland or somewhere else to build it without taking dozens of little farms and homes? This is some of the best farm land in the whole world, as Papa said. If the rest of the world is going to eat and smoke tobacco, somebody has to farm," she added, remembering a thought in an F.C.X. speech she had made.

"We're selfish, perhaps, but we love our farms and homes like you love your family and the things you own."

Melody paused. Big tears had formed in the corners of her eyes and were running down the sides of her nose. Her voice trembled as she spoke again. "If you can find another way, please don't take our farms from us—no matter how much money you plan to pay for them. I thank you."

She turned around slowly, wiping her face with her sweaty, trembling hand, and walked down the long dark aisle. At the back of the courtroom, she paused. She couldn't sit down again. She must go to the truck. Papa had parked it nearby. She could find it easily.

The truck was hot inside, even with the windows rolled down. Melody closed the door and buried her burning face in her lap.

When Mr. Nottoman got to the truck a few minutes later, she was still sitting there, tears staining the lap of her yellow dress. Her father patted her on the shoulder. Of course he wouldn't scold her in town. She could not bear to look at him.

He cranked the truck and started toward home. Melody wished that he would say something.

86

Finally, he handed her his handkerchief and said, "Sit up, little friend. You'll miss all the scenery."

At home again, Melody went immediately to the well and drew water to wash her face. When she started in the back door, she heard her father telling her mother in very low tones that Melody had made a speech at the hearing.

"What did she say, John?" her mother was asking.

"Oh, about the same things we decided for me to try to say."

"I guess she's a little of both of us, you reckon?" Her mother chuckled.

"Yes, I guess she is, at that."

Melody turned, went down the doorsteps, and, followed by Pup-Pup, went behind the corncrib, where she sat down on an old cinder block she had put there in her dollhouse days and cried until she could cry no more. She wasn't afraid of Papa, she told herself finally, not even at the courthouse. The tears had to do with losing Big Oaks to the airport people. Nothing could possibly be worse than that—not for the moment anyway!

CHAPTER 11

ON THE WEDNESDAY following the airport hearing, excitement caused Melody to awaken before dawn. Today was the day of the barbecue. This was the happiest day that one could imagine. Or was it? Maybe it had a competitor, the opening of the market, tomorrow.

Only a faint hint of light was showing through the windows. Melody turned over, her eyes still closed, full of anticipation. The door squeaked, and Melody turned her head toward the sound.

It was Teddy clad in pajamas, carrying his favorite old teddy bear. Faded and somewhat soiled in places, with both eyes missing and a leg "injured" from wear and tear, the teddy bear was essential to a good night's sleep, according to Teddy's thinking.

"What's the matter, Teddy?" questioned Melody.

"Nothin', Melody. I just wanted to see you. I'm just about woke up, but not quite."

"You are still sleepy," said Melody, fluffing her pillow. "Here, get up here beside me and go back to sleep."

"I can't sleep, Melody. I tried."

Melody lay very still, hoping that Teddy would go back to sleep.

After a few moments, Teddy, realizing that Melody was not asleep, turned toward her and said, "Melody, let's get up. I bet Jake's done started cooking that barbecue."

"No, he hasn't." Melody laughed. "He won't start that until about noon. The barbecue won't be ready until late this afternoon."

"But I heard somebody outside. I bet it was Jake. I bet he got hungry and started cookin' that pig already."

"No, you're just like me—excited, that's all. You're just hearing things. Go to sleep."

Teddy half-closed his eyes. Melody looked at him in his little-boy deception. Again she wondered if his ear would really be a handicap. But the pain was real, the threat of deafness was constant, and there was so little money in the sugar bag.

"How long does it take for an answer to a prayer to come? Will a dream ever come true?" she asked herself in the silence, as she stared at the ceiling.

A big lump came in her throat. The tears started to form. When she sniffled slightly, Teddy turned to her and said, "Goodness, Melody, are you cryin' over me 'cause I woke you up? I'm sorry, Melody. I didn't mean to wake you up. I'll go back to my bed."

"No, don't. It's O.K. We're both going to get up soon. There's so much to be done to get ready for the barbecue."

89

"Oh, boy! I like getting up," said Teddy, jumping out of bed, " 'specially when it's barbecue day. But you don't like gettin' up no time, do you, Melody?"

"Well, maybe on a good day, when we're not putting in tobacco and I have a nice little boy to call me. Now you go to your room and get dressed. I'll come in there in a few minutes and help you with the buttons."

"Okee-dokee. Then we can go to the shelter to see if it really was Jake I heard!"

In the kitchen Mrs. Nottoman was busily preparing breakfast. Melody stopped just long enough to say "Good morning" and "How are you?" on her way through the kitchen. "I'll be back to help you in a minute, Mama. Teddy and I want to go to the barn. Don't cook much breakfast for me. I'm saving space for this evening's feast," shouted Melody as she went to Teddy's room.

When she and Teddy arrived at the barn, Jake was busy with a shovel digging a rectangular hole in the center of the shelter.

"Even if it rains, this little ol' pig is still going to cook. Right, Jake?" said Melody, lifting one foot of the pig that had, the day before, been firmly packed for safe-keeping in a tub of ice.

"Yes, ma'am. We gonna' cook dat pig come rain or shine," replied Jake.

"Since he's chilled, maybe frozen, you're going to

have to put him on a little early, aren't you, Jake?"

"Oh, no." Jake laughed. "He'll be plenty cooked by dis evenin'. I promise you dat."

"I'll take him for dinner if it's O.K. with you. I just can't wait."

Jake smiled and kept on digging. The iron bars, needed to hold the wire on which the pig would lie, stood beside the barn.

"I can't imagine Buster preferring to go swimming with the boys instead of staying here for this barbecue, can you, Jake?"

"Well, Miss Melody. You knows how boys is. Dey thinks anything like a party is silly," said Jake.

"But this is not a party; it's a feast—a barbecue feast. It's the best eating in the whole United States world!"

"I agrees. I sho' agrees, Miss Melody."

"Well, just let me know if you need me. The sooner this evening comes, the better I will like it."

"I'll help you, too, Jake, if you need me. I can be a barbecue-cooker, too," offered Teddy.

"We might be callin' on our little tobacco-picker. Don't you git too far away," said Jake.

"O.K., I won't," said Teddy, with a big grin.

After lunch, Alice-Cora-Jane came to help Mrs. Nottoman with the preparation for the barbecue.

Alice-Cora-Jane was as large as any woman could be, but she was as kind and good and as smart as she was large. No one knew how much she weighed because no ordinary scales would register her weight. Her eyes were large; so was her mouth, but she always spoke with a soft voice, even when correcting her children; yet she said more with her eyes than she did with her words. It was well known that she was the best cook in the county.

Melody wondered what her hair really looked like. Her trademark, perhaps, besides her immaculate house and even cleaner children, was the large blue bandana handkerchief, patterned with white stars, that she always wore, tied turban style, around her head. Melody had often told Alice-Cora-Jane that she had stars in her crown, even more than those in the blue bandana.

Alice-Cora-Jane's being there gave Melody an additional feeling of freedom. Now she could stay outside at the shelter and smell the barbecue even better. She could even pull a browned rib or a crisp piece of skin from the sizzling pig. Nothing was better.

Little Moses, still wearing his bandages, was sitting on a cinder block beside the barn door, where he could watch every move Jake made. The ability to cook a good barbecue was a skill handed down from one generation to another. Not everyone could cook a pig just right. One had to know exactly what kind of wood to use. The wood had to burn just enough, but not too much. The pig had to cook just enough, but not too much, before he was turned over. One had to know exactly when to add the vinegar and salt and pepper and how much. Little Moses watched every act. Alice-Cora-Jane had dressed him early, immaculate in every detail, so that he could come early to enjoy his apprenticeship.

When Melody arrived, he stood up.

"Hello there, Little Moses. You learning to be a pig-cooker?"

"Yes, Miss Melody," he answered.

"We certainly have missed you during this mad to-bacco season. In fact, I don't know how we made it without you."

"Thank you, Miss Melody. I missed y'all, too."

Melody pulled a piece of tender barbecue meat to sample it. "Bet this is tenderloin. Best part of the hog. Right, Jake?"

"Any barbecue meat is good to me, Miss Melody," answered Jake.

Abraham and Teddy arrived with a tobacco truck loaded with watermelons fresh from the patch.

"Good evening, Abraham. Hiya, Teddy, ol' boy. You'll have to sell those watermelons. Nobody's going to eat melons when barbecue is around," teased Melody.

"You might be right." Abraham laughed.

"We got the biggest ones in the patch, Melody. See, I put my mark on this one when it was little, and now it's growed real big just for today," said Teddy, pointing proudly at the X he had carved on the watermelon when he and Melody had first gone to the patch long before there was any hope that the melons might be ripe.

Teddy, smiling big enough to show the hole left by a front tooth lost as the result of a fall, nudged close to Melody and said, "You ain't never smelt a man that smells as good as me, have you, Melody?" He was so fascinated by his father's after-shave lotion that he had asked his mother to rub some on his face when he returned to the house at lunch. Melody smiled, tightened her grip around his shoulders, and pulled him to her.

"All dressed up for the barbecue, eh, boy?" teased Melody.

"Sure am," responded Teddy, returning to the pile of burning wood in the field near the shelter. He was attempting to stir it with a tobacco stick so that it would be ready for Jake to use when he needed it in the barbecue pit.

Mrs. Nottoman called from the edge of the yard. "Melody, come get the paper to put on the trucks. Time to fix the tables. Ask Jake how long it will be before we can bring the rest of the food."

As she left to go to the house, Jake assured her that the barbecue would be done soon. Melody skipped for joy as she carried the good news to her mother.

94

When she returned to the barn, all of Alice-Cora-Jane's and Jake's children were there, their teeth sparkling through smiles and their eyes glistening with excitement.

"One, two, three, four, five, six, seven, eight, nine: It's always good luck if you speak in a rhyme," teased Melody as she greeted them. "Hope all of you are happy and hungry. Say, Martha, give me a hand with this paper. We've got to cover the tobacco trucks for tables so we can bring all that good food that Mama and Alice-Cora-Jane are cooking."

Martha came forth quickly. Mary, determined not to be left out, joined her.

Methusalah, a fat, dimpled eight-month-old boy with dozens of ringlets of curly black hair, seemed to have caught the spirit of the occasion too as he gurgled from his pallet at one side of the shelter. Joseph and Aaron looked as if they would burst with happiness.

Isaac had arrived also. He was helping Jake lift the pig to see whether it was burning. From time to time, the two of them stuck forks into the meat to test it for tenderness. From time to time, they added vinegar and salt and seasonings.

Mr. Nottoman greeted the group with "Well, well, how are my little tobacco hands today? Glad to see you all."

He surveyed the group. "Jake, I've never seen such dressed-up children. You'd think they were going to church."

Jake looked pleased. The children looked at each other and smiled.

Mr. Nottoman and Jake were whispering something. Melody knew it must be about the barbecue.

It was. Mr. Nottoman turned around and said, "All of you that are big enough to 'tote' a pot or bowl, go to the house and start bringing the other food. Jake and Isaac and I are going to start cutting up this barbecue right now."

CHAPTER 12

ABRAHAM, JOSEPH, MARY, MARTHA, and Little Moses, who said, "I can tote somethin' light," joined Melody for the trip to the house. Alice-Cora-Jane met them at the back door and handed them boxes, pots, bowls, and pans full of every food imaginable.

"It'll be like Christmas jist seein' what's in all dese, won't it, Miss Melody?" said Little Moses.

"Sure will. I'm so hungry I think I could eat every bit of all of it."

The little band formed a follow-the-leader line back to the barn. Everyone watched his step and walked slowly, as Alice-Cora-Jane had advised.

Pup-Pup saw them coming, stood up, and came toward them, wagging his tail.

"You smell this good food a-coming, eh, Pup-Pup?" said Melody. "You're leaving something better than what we're bringing—better to you at least. Haven't they given you a barbecue bone yet?"

Jake heard her. "Oh, yes. He's had so many bones he's tired of 'em a'ready."

"Be glad when I can say the same," said Melody, as

she and the others set the containers on the tobacco trucks.

Melody lifted the white cover from the top of the huge wooden tub filled with chopped barbecue. "Look, look," she said to Mary. "Have you ever seen such a sight?"

"No, I sho' ain't, an' it smells better'n anything I ever smelt," quickly answered Mary.

"Where are Mama and Alice-Cora-Jane?" questioned Mr. Nottoman.

"I'll go get them," answered Melody. "No, here they come now."

Mrs. Nottoman and Alice-Cora-Jane, bringing paper plates, cups, napkins, and wooden forks, joined the happy group. They checked the containers brought by the children a few moments earlier.

Teddy could contain himself no longer. "Ain't this nice, Mama? I'm so happy I think I'll bust."

"I agrees, but I'd rather bust from overeatin'," said Martha.

Mrs. Nottoman smiled at both of them.

"Let's all stand for the blessing," suggested Mr. Nottoman.

Everyone stood, bowed his head, and closed his eyes—all except Joseph. Abraham nudged Joseph's arm quickly with his elbow. "Shet yore eyes, Joseph. You ain't s'posed to look at Mr. Nottoman when he prays," said Abraham in whispered tones.

Mr. Nottoman began:

"Our Father,

"We thank Thee for this good day that has brought us to this good occasion.

"We thank Thee for all Thy goodness toward us— for keeping us through this busy season, for good health, for the rain and the sunshine, and our crops—and especially for healing Little Moses.

"We thank Thee for working with us as we worked together in these families to provide things needed.

"We thank Thee for our friends. We ask that we shall learn to live peacefully with all mankind.

"Bless now this food to the nourishment of our bodies and us to Thy service.

Amen"

There was a moment of silence. Then Mr. Nottoman lifted his head, smiled, and said, "Who will be first? Just who will be first?"

"Mama," said Teddy, " 'cause she's the best Mama in the whole world."

Applause rose from the group.

"Thank you, Teddy. You and the others are too good to me. But I'm not going to make a speech. I'm just not a speechmaker, but I appreciate the applause."

They all laughed.

"No, you menfolks go first. Really. I'll help fix plates for the little ones," insisted Mrs. Nottoman.

"An' I'll help you," said Alice-Cora-Jane, coming forward, uncovering all the "surprise" dishes.

And so, again, the famished little tobacco-putting-in crew made a follow-the-leader line around the table, putting a little of everything on each plate—barbecue, slaw, baked sweet potatoes, corn bread, snap beans, butter beans, Brunswick stew, pickles, corn, and sandwiches of all kinds.

"No space for cake or cookies or sweets now," commented Melody, with her plate piled high.

"Or watermelons," sighed Abraham.

"I's seen an' et watermelon all summer," said Joseph. "But some o' dis good food stuff I ain't never seen, or 'specially et befo'."

"Just help yourself, Joseph. There's more than enough," offered Mr. Nottoman.

Except for the sound of the rainfrogs and an occasional call of the whippoorwill, there was an almost complete silence as each one found a comfortable place to set his plate and Pepsi. Everyone was too busy eating to speak.

"Plenty more on the table," called Mrs. Nottoman.

"Mama, you haven't eaten a thing yourself," said Melody.

"I'm going to right now. Don't worry about me."

Hands became greasy, white shirts and pressed trousers among Alice-Cora-Jane's crew began to show signs of spillings and soiled spots, but there were smiles on every face.

Everyone, young and old, ate until he could eat no more.

"That's the best barbecue in the whole world," complimented Melody to Jake.

"Thank you, Miss Melody. I enjoyed cookin' it."

"That makes a difference in the cooking, I believe," added Mr. Nottoman.

"Anyone for more cake?" questioned Mrs. Nottoman.

"Or more watermelon?" added Mr. Nottoman.

When it was agreed that no one could possibly eat any more, the follow-the-leader line was again formed, at Mrs. Nottoman's suggestion, so that the dishes and left-over food could be taken to the house. Everyone seemed too full and too lazy to budge, but the food had to be moved before it was ruined by flies, ants, and other insects.

"We'll play a game and burn some of these calories when we get back," suggested Melody. "If we don't hurry, it will be too dark."

"It will have to be a sit-down game for me, 'cause I is de fattest one. I's too full to walk, more 'specially to run," commented Martha.

Mrs. Nottoman, who had gone along with Alice-

Cora-Jane and the others, held the back door open as each one filed in and put his box or dish or pan on the bench or table, wherever there was space.

"Mighty good food, Mrs. Nottoman," complimented Joseph.

The others added their words of praise.

"And I thank you. Glad you enjoyed it," responded Mrs. Nottoman.

It was beginning to get dark.

"We almost need a lantern," commented Melody. "Watch out for toad-frogs and other things that might be hopping or crawling around."

"My goodness! You scares me to death. I's skeered to death o' snakes, an' dey're a crawlin' thing," said Mary, coming close to Melody.

"Oh, don't be afraid. No snakes around here—maybe," teased Melody.

"Look!" screamed Melody. "Smoke! There's smoke at Mr. Ezra's. Goodness! Papa! Papa!" she yelled.

Isaac heard her and ran from under the shelter to see the smoke.

"Mr. Nottoman! Mr. Nottoman! Come here! Dey's a fire at Mr. Ezra's house. Look! Look! Mr. Nottoman. Somethin' is a-burnin' up!"

Mr. Nottoman, by this time, had seen the smoke. "There is a fire! Start the truck, Isaac. I'll be on as

soon as I tell Mrs. Nottoman to call the fire depart-
ment!"

"I can't go up der, Mr. Nottoman. Mr. Ezra will
shoot me down sho'!"

"Goodness, Isaac. This is no time for such talk. Go!
It will take all of us to put out the fire!"

Isaac hesitantly turned to go toward the truck, as
Melody and her father ran as fast as they could toward
the house. Mrs. Nottoman was standing in the kitchen
door.

"What is it?" she called.

"A fire over at Mr. Ezra's. Will you call the fire truck
and then ring the dinner bell?" yelled Mr. Nottoman.

"I dread to hear the bell. Bells sure do sound weird at
night—like death or something. Papa told me once that
old folks used to always ring dinner bells, slow and
loud, when someone died," recalled Melody as she and
Mr. Nottoman ran to the truck.

It was the corn barn. The smoke was getting heavier
and blacker.

"My goodness, how on earth could that have caught
on fire?" thought Melody as she and her father approached. "Mr. Ezra could have been right. Someone
could have stolen his corn and then set fire to the barn."

When they arrived, someone was screaming and crying.

"I can't see who it is, but it must be Mrs. Ezra. Listen, Papa."

"Somebody come here! Somebody help me," Mrs. Ezra screamed. "Ezra's burning up! Lord Jesus, somebody get him out! The door's locked and we can't never get him out!"

Melody put her arm around Mrs. Ezra. "Lord, child, Ezra's in there with his foot caught in the hayloft! His lantern turned over and fell down and started a fire right under him! Lord, child, what are we going to do? Ezra's going to burn to death and he ain't prepared to die."

Melody ran to the door. Mr. Nottoman and Isaac were already there.

"Locked!" said Papa hopelessly.

"Mr. Nottoman, ain't dere another winder or a door somewhere?"

"All barred up with iron bars. We'll have to knock off some boards or something. Anybody know where there is a crowbar?" shouted Mr. Nottoman amid the confusion.

"Wait! I know! Here, Isaac, Papa! Come with me!"

Rapidly, Melody led them to a small hole in the back of the barn. The boards around it were rotten and jagged. Smoke was pouring out. Melody put her mouth next to the hole and shouted, "We're here, Mr. Ezra! We're here! We're coming in!"

She moved away from the hole quickly and gasped for breath. In another second she and Isaac and Mr. Nottoman began tearing off the boards with their bare hands. Mr. Nottoman pulled her away.

"No, Papa! I've got to help. Please!"

In a time too short to measure, the hole was big enough for Isaac to go through. Taking a tow bag to fight the flames, Isaac crawled inside through the black smoke, his way lighted only by the flames.

"You wait here, Mr. Nottoman; I can git him, I knows I can," said Isaac, as he moved inside.

Once more, Melody placed her mouth against the opening and shouted through the smoke, "We're coming, Mr. Ezra. We're coming!"

Then, before her father could stop her, she crawled through the hole. Inside, she fought her way through the smoke, blowing and fanning uselessly with her hands. Stumbling across the corn, she reached the locked door. Her eyes watered and burned as she searched desperately for the latch, hoping that the door could be opened from the inside.

In the darkness, she heard Isaac fumbling toward Mr. Ezra, who was moaning. "Isaac's getting you, Mr. Ezra. He's coming to get you safe." Smoke filled her eyes and mouth.

"Oh, God, help us," begged Melody. "Help me to find the latch."

Mr. Nottoman was at the hole yelling, "Melody, where are you? Are you all right? Answer me!"

Her father was frantic, but she could not afford to eat enough smoke to answer him. She must save her breath in case Mr. Ezra and Isaac needed her. Smoke was getting into her lungs, and she felt dizzy.

Just then she slipped on an ear of corn, and her hand fell against the latch. Immediately, she jerked the door partway open.

"Isaac, Mr. Ezra! Are you coming? Can you see the light? I've got the door open. Come to the light. Can I help?"

"We's comin', Miss Melody, soon as I can git Mr. Ezra's leg unhung. I don't want to break it, but it's hung bad. You git out o' here." Isaac coughed.

When Melody heard Isaac coming, she slipped out the door.

"I's got him. Git out o' here, Miss Melody, git out o' here!" screamed Isaac, not knowing that she was safe.

"Are you all right, Melody?" asked her father anxiously as he came running around the barn. "What on earth were you thinking about?"

"I'm O. K., Papa. Really I am."

Mrs. Ezra was standing a few feet away, hysterical with fear. "Isaac is getting him," comforted Melody. "He'll bring him out safe and sound! Don't you worry!"

Mrs. Ezra was trembling. She was not much taller

than Melody and not any larger. Melody could have counted Mrs. Ezra's ribs with her hand as her fingers hugged her to try to comfort her. Her straight gray hair hung in her face and she smelled smoky and hot.

"I wanted to get him out, but I couldn't find a way. He's going to die, Melody! I know he is," wailed Mrs. Ezra.

Neighbors were coming up the path—on foot, in cars, on trucks, and even one man on a mule.

"See, a lot of help is coming. We'll get him out now. See, all your friends are coming to help you," said Melody, her own voice trembling.

"We ain't got no friends. You know we ain't."

"But you have. See, just look at all of them."

"You just don't know how it is to live all alone and unloved, Melody. It's the worst thing in the whole world," sobbed Mrs. Ezra. "Melody, do you smell flesh burning?"

"Oh, no, no, Mrs. Ezra. It's only lightwood timber burning," comforted Melody, uncertain of the truth of the statement.

People were everywhere. Some were drawing water, some filling and passing buckets, some standing with hands in front of their faces to ward off the heat.

Suddenly, almost like a ghost, Isaac appeared, carrying Mr. Ezra, who hung limply in Isaac's huge arms. Isaac's shirt and trousers were torn to shreds.

"Lord, he's dead! I know he's dead," screamed Mrs. Ezra, falling flat on her face as she leaned forward to touch her husband.

"Quick, 'fore she faints. Tell 'er he ain't dead, yet. Tell her, Miss Melody!"

She had already fainted. "Here, somebody," yelled Melody. "Help me with Mrs. Ezra. She's fainted!"

Several men came to the rescue. They lifted Mrs. Ezra's frail body and started to the house. Melody followed.

"Say, somebody," said Mr. Nottoman, "we've got to have a car to take this man to Wilson. He's almost burned to death."

"Here, put him in mine," offered Mr. Freeman, a neighbor. "I'll be glad to take him. Somebody will have to go along and hold him, though."

Mr. Nottoman opened the back door of Mr. Freeman's car.

"Mr. Nottoman, what does I do with him? His burnt flesh might stick to de seat if I lays him down!" said Isaac.

"Can you get in and keep holding him, Isaac?"

"Yas, suh, I thinks so. I'll try," said Isaac, who was already seated before he had finished talking.

"You just hold him as comfortable as you can, Isaac. I'll sit in the front seat. Looks like they have enough help with the fire. The barn's going to be a total loss anyway. Yonder comes the fire truck at last."

"Fires really are bad things," said Mr. Freeman as he drove down the path. "Fires and floods and earthquakes and hurricanes and hailstorms and things. It's hard to understand why they have to be."

"I don't know," said Mr. Nottoman. "But I always say that if no lives are lost, all other losses seem unimportant."

"You're right, John, and Mr. Ezra sure owes his life to Isaac and Melody. She's a fine young'un, John."

"Thank you, Freeman."

"You're a hero now, Isaac," said Mr. Freeman. "A real hero."

"I thanks you. I thanks you. But I ain't done no mo' than any man woulda' done in my place," replied Isaac in a choked voice.

Isaac sat very still, holding Mr. Ezra as carefully as he could. Somewhere, in all the confusion, he kept trying to piece together something that Alice-Cora-Jane had taught him about no greater love than that a man lay down his life for a friend. When he could not make the words fit, he bowed his head and said silently, "Dear Gawd, help dis pore burnin' man. Please, Gawd. Don't let 'im die! An' thank you fo' dat hole dat Miss Melody knowed 'bout an' showed us an' fo' unlockin' de door for us. If it hadn't been fo' dese, we'd-a never got in in time to save dis pore burnin' man."

CHAPTER 13

THE MOON STILL PROVIDED LIGHT for Melody as she made her way home from Mrs. Ezra's the next morning at four o'clock. Everything was covered with a heavy August dew. Even the dirt was damp enough to stick to her feet as she hurried to Big Oaks.

"I've never seen so many car tracks," said Melody to herself. "Must have been a hundred folks coming in and out of this path last night. That sure was something. Barn a-blazing, Mrs. Ezra a-screaming, Mr. Ezra a-burning. Goodness, that was a night! I know I'll remember it as long as I live. Seems impossible that last night could have been so noisy and dreadful and this morning could be so peaceful and still. It's like the calm after that hailstorm. Life sure is strange that way," Melody thought. "Everything gets so troubled and so mixed up and then, all of a sudden, everything gets back right again. Mrs. Ezra's resting all right since the doctor gave her some medicine. But I wonder about poor old Mr. Ezra. I wonder how he is. He sure was a burnt-up looking man. If he lives, I wonder how much he'll have to suffer. I know how bad it hurts just to burn my finger when I'm helping Mama cook."

When Melody came to the curve in the road so that she could see Big Oaks clearly, she hastened her steps.

"My goodness! I had almost forgotten that this is tobacco market opening day! Yonder's Papa and Isaac already tightening the canvas on the truck. I must hurry or they'll think I'm not going with them. Oh, this is about the best day in the United States world!"

When she reached Mr. Nottoman and Isaac, her father immediately asked, "Melody, where on earth have you been?"

"Didn't Mama tell you? I spent the night with Mrs. Ezra. She wanted me to. I sent word to Mama by one of the neighbors. It was all right with you, wasn't it, Papa?"

"If you behaved yourself."

"I did, Papa. I'm getting too old to do otherwise. I'm almost a teen-ager."

"How is Mrs. Ezra?" asked Mr. Nottoman anxiously.

"Oh, she's fine—or maybe I'd better say better—since the doctor gave her some medicine and since I told her that Mr. Ezra wasn't dead. He's not dead, is he, Papa?"

"I hope not, Melody, but he's a mighty sick man. The doctor said he had third degree burns and they're mighty deep and bad."

"Goodness, Papa. You really and truly think he's going to be all right?"

"It's too early to tell. We've got to go by to see him this morning as soon as the tobacco's sold. Now get dressed. We've got to get there and get these lugs unloaded if we want to make today's sale."

When Mr. Nottoman and Isaac and Melody were well on their way to Wilson, Melody, after a long silence, said, "You know something, Papa. I'm getting hot trembles in my stomach. It's done'n passed the butterfly stage."

"Melody, you do exaggerate a little at times, don't you?"

"But, Papa, it's the truth. But you must be excited, too. After all that hard work, here we go to good old Wilson to sell the golden leaves for little old greenback dollars—or I mean for a check that you can swap for little old greenbacks."

"Melody, you talk so much about becoming a teenager that I hesitate to mention it. But you will be growing up soon—and fast. As for me, I don't have much education. Had to stop in the ninth grade when your grandpa Nottoman had his stroke."

"But you read a lot, don't you, Papa? Is that where you learned so much?"

"I don't know much, Melody. But what I do know came mostly from reading and listening to the radio and talking with people. School is the best opportunity for an education, perhaps. It isn't the only one. But

114

there's one thing I've observed. We—meaning you and I—we use too much slang in our talking. Now when you get to be a teen-ager and especially a late teen-ager who's becoming a lady . . ."

"My goodness, Papa. Don't you worry 'bout me. You'd be surprised to know how well I can talk when I want to. I've been to school, you know, and I've observed quite a bit. But you know something, Papa? If you'll trust me when I say I know better, I'd kinda' like to go on talking for a while to match my blue jeans and the tobacco."

"O.K. But I did want to mention it. A young lady is judged very often by the way she talks."

"Say," said Melody rather apologetically to Isaac, "you can say something."

"I was just listenin', Miss Melody. Like your papa says, folkses can learn a whole lot by jist listenin'. Dat's 'bout de best way I knows of to learn, an' I was just thinkin', de last time I come along dis road, I was a-sittin' in de back seat o' Mr. Freeman's car a-holdin' pore ol' burnt-up Mr. Ezra. Dat shore am a pitiful human bein'.'"

"He sure is, Isaac, and I know he appreciates what you did for him."

"He prob'ly don't even know, Miss Melody, an' don't you tell him. Just let things be as dey is."

"He already knows, Isaac. Last night when he regained consciousness, he asked who got him out of the barn and we told him," said Mr. Nottoman.

"What did he say, Papa?"

"Well, he mumbled, 'Tell Isaac and Melody thank you,' and then he blacked out again."

"You know what, Miss Melody an' Mr. Nottoman. Maybe I shouldn't say dis, but last night when we was a-comin' to Wilson, de moon was a-shinin' beams in at de winder an' I was a-lookin' down at Mr. Ezra an' I says to myself, 'Mr. Ezra, yore face am as black as mine now.' Jist like six foot of earth makes us all de same size, dat fire done made Mr. Ezra an' me de same color."

"It is all right for you to say that, Isaac," said Melody. "He sure was a scarred old man."

"One question," said Mr. Nottoman. "How did you know about the hole in the back of the barn?"

"We found it the other day when all of us went to the store for candy and I was trying to prove that Mr. Ezra's land wasn't poisoned."

"It sho' was a good thing to know about las' night. It sho' was!" said Isaac, shaking his head.

CHAPTER 14

INSIDE BRIGHT GOLD WAREHOUSE, Melody was sitting on the hood watching the surrounding activities. Mr. Nottoman stood beside the truck.

"They bring tobacco in here on everything, don't they, Papa?"

"Oh, yes. Pickups, trailers, big trucks."

"And even the mule and wagon," added Melody.

"Right you are."

"And look at the people, Papa. I didn't know so many tourists would be here so early. It's just after sunrise."

"Many tourists travel early, and they stop at Bright Gold. They come in here all day long from places as far away as Maine and Florida."

"There must be some of everybody here, Papa." Melody saw farmers, many in overalls, some in coveralls. Men in pressed trousers. Men in sweat shirts, others in T-shirts, others with no shirts at all. "And look at the women, Papa. Some of 'em dressed up, some of 'em dressed down, just like me! Look, Papa. There comes Isaac."

"Ready to unload, Mr. Nottoman?"

"Guess we're already overdue. But we have to wait our turn. Already three rows ahead of us."

"She sho' is fillin' up today. Gonna be a big sale fo' de openin'," said Isaac.

"You mean they're going to fill up this whole great big warehouse before the sale starts, Papa?"

"Why, no, Melody. And if they did, they wouldn't sell it all today. Each warehouse can sell only a limited number of baskets each day. Keeps the redrying plants from being overcrowded!"

"Will ours be sold today, Papa?"

"Oh, yes. You just stand aside awhile so Isaac and I can slip these bundles off the grading sticks and pile them on the baskets."

Melody watched closely as they filled the baskets and gave each basket a tag telling the pounds, owner's name, and farmer's number. "Look, Papa. Ours starts with the first basket on the fourth row," she said, as Isaac pushed the basket away. "Be sold about what time?"

"About ten, I'd say."

"You know something, Papa. I'll never hear the last of this, but I believe I'll just curl up in the front of this old pickup and take a little snooze until the sale starts. I didn't get much sleep after the fire. Will you wake me up about nine o'clock, Papa?"

"Oh, yes. You'll enjoy the sale more if you're not

sleepy. When we get all the tobacco unloaded, I'll move the truck to the other side of the warehouse so it won't be in the way and it will be quieter for you to sleep."

"Oh, thank you, Papa."

"This sure is a big place," Melody thought, as she curled up on the truck seat. "Big enough for tourists to tour, farmers to unload tobacco, cars and wagons and trucks to move around, and big enough for little ol' me to go to sleep."

About 8:45 Melody was awakened by what she called her mental alarm clock. "Just set your mind to do something, and that's all you need," she had said. "Only thing, when it comes to getting up in the morning, I refuse to set any kind of clock!"

She sat up, yawned, rubbed her eyes, and looked out the window of the truck. Her father was coming toward her. He saw her and yelled, "Come on. Time for the sale to start!"

Melody jumped out of the truck, skipped to her father, and took him by the hand. "Land sakes, Papa. I never saw so many people. Hundreds of them. Reckon we can get a standing place near our tobacco when it's sold?"

"Maybe."

"Look, Papa. Some men are lining up on each side of the first row of tobacco. What's all that about?"

"See those first two men on the right? Well, they're

brothers. They've been in the tobacco warehouse business as long as I can remember. One of them starts the sale and the other one runs the sale. See the second one pulling bundles from each pile? He's trying to show the tobacco to the buyers, hoping they'll like the color and quality and texture and buy it. The third man is the auctioneer. The man behind the auctioneer is the ticket marker. When a company buys a basket of tobacco, he marks the ticket telling what company bought it and how much was paid for it. He may become an auctioneer, a buyer, or a warehouseman, or he may leave the tobacco business altogether. Many of our most capable, and often richest, tobacco men started out as farmers or ticket markers."

"Really, Papa? You mean he didn't go to college to learn all this?"

"Oh, no. He could have, but in tobacco most things are learned through experience."

"Who are the nine men on the other side of the row, Papa?"

"Oh, they're buyers. You know, on the radio you've heard advertisements by Reynolds Tobacco Company that makes Camel Cigarettes, American Tobacco Company that makes Lucky Strikes, and Liggett and Myers that makes Chesterfields. There are also others like Imperial, Export, and Brown-Williamson. Well, each company has a buyer here who buys tobacco for his company."

"One more question, Papa. Who is the man over there on the third row? He's putting something on the tickets."

"Oh, he's a government grader. He labels the tobacco as to type and then writes down how much the government will pay for that particular basket in case the buyers don't want that certain kind of curing. Now, you listen to the man who starts the sale. He will say—well, let's say fifty cents. That will be about three cents above the government support price. If the buyers don't want to pay fifty cents for it, either the warehouse will buy it for that price or stabilization will buy it for forty-seven cents. You see, it's as simple as that, and the farmer is assured of at least a fair price for his tobacco. We've had this plan since about 1946, I believe."

"America sure is a wonderful old free country, isn't she, Papa? She reaches from the tobacco fields of Wilson County to the top of the Empire State Building, just trying to help her people."

"She's a great country, Melody. And as you grow older, you'll learn to love and appreciate her more."

"Listen, Papa. That first man has said something. Come, let's move closer. Goodness, that's a loud auctioneer. Listen at him, Papa. First he sounds like he's singing. Then he sounds like a machine gun. Doesn't he ever stop to breathe?"

"He has to talk fast. Sometimes he sells over forty baskets a minute. Sensible or not, that's sweet music to these farmers' ears."

"Those buyers use funny signals, don't they, Papa?"

"Oh, yes, sometimes they nod their head, raise their foot, snap their fingers, tip their hat. The auctioneer knows their sign."

"I sure am getting nervous. Aren't you, Papa? What if ours doesn't sell good, Papa, after all that hard work and getting up early in the morning and everything!"

"It's just a chance we have to take. We'll have to wait and see."

"It's hopeless for me, Papa. I can't understand a thing that auctioneer says, and I'll get mashed to pieces in that crowd. I think I'll just sit down on this jack and wait till they get to our tobacco. O.K.?"

"O.K. now, but don't go away."

"Don't worry. I won't go away, not until we get our greenback check!"

Melody sat down and watched the crowd following the auctioneer and the buyers examining the sold tobacco. Behind the crowd walked two ticket men, figuring each man's sale simultaneously to avoid any error. Already men were moving the sold baskets of tobacco to trucks each parked in a certain doorway over which was written the name of its company. The trucks would take the tobacco to the factories or processing plants, where it would be redried, packed in hogsheads or large barrels, and sent away for storage to sleep and age, later to be made into cigarettes, snuff, chewing tobacco, cigars, or perhaps exported to foreign countries.

A young woman representing the Salvation Army whispered something to each farmer as his tobacco was weighed. Most of the time, she lifted a bundle or two from each farmer's basket.

A little colored boy of about three came from the direction of the concession stand licking a cone of dripping ice cream. A blind man led by a seeing-eye dog came to the door and stopped to listen. A mother went toward the rest room with her crying baby. A confused drunk appeared from among the crowd, was tapped on the shoulder by a policeman, and was led away, not without resistance and great commotion. A stray dog wandered in, glanced at the crowd, stuck his tail under his legs, and ran out again. The man who was running the sale adjusted the sweat rag on his forehead. A tall blonde in a tight skirt and a fitted blouse caught for a moment the attention of the crowd. A farmer came by in patched coveralls. "It's just not fair. They might as well have gone to my barn and stole my tobacco," he said.

"Mine didn't do too bad. I didn't see your tobacco.

But, as usual, the quality of most of the lugs is poor. Buyers just naturally wait for the body tobacco," said his companion, who looked as if he were in less need of money than his friend.

"This is a little world within itself," thought Melody, as she noticed three tourists who stood gazing, shaking their heads.

The sale was moving fast. They were on the third row. Melody stood on her tiptoes and scanned the crowd for Papa. "There he is, engrossed in the sale. Reckon he's going to take notice of how everybody's is selling so he can be sure he gets a fair price," said Melody to herself.

Mr. Nottoman left the crowd and came toward Melody.

"Gee, Papa, I don't think I can stand it. I think I'm going to have a heart attack. How on earth can you stand it?"

"Well, I don't feel so relaxed myself. But good quality tobacco is selling above last year's price, and that's always a good sign."

"Look, Papa. Some of the tobacco. They aren't moving it away. The farmers are doing something to the tags."

"Some of the farmers are dissatisfied. They're turning tags. They just take the ticket out of the little slot in the stick and fold it or tear off the price and the name of the company. If a farmer turns tags on his tobacco, he must repack it, reweigh it, place it in another row, have the government grader reconsider it, and have the buyers bid on it again."

"That's a lot of work, Papa."

"Yes, it is. And sometimes it sells for a higher price and sometimes for a lower price. It's just a chance the farmer takes."

As Melody walked around, looking at the tobacco and observing carefully all the activities, a feeling of defeat and sickness kept swelling in her. She and Buster would have no tobacco to sell this year, she kept remembering. If only the storm had not come! Papa had lost the tips off his acres, too, as well as the primings next to the tips. But he had said that the Good Lord would provide, and that was sufficient consolation— for the moment, at least.

The auction team was over halfway down the third row. "I'll tell you, Papa, I don't mean to be a coward and desert you, but I'd rather not go with you to see our tobacco sold."

"Oh, come on. Just take my hand and listen real hard. If the auctioneer says anything above fifty, that's real good today."

"But what if I can't understand, Papa? I tell you

what. If it's selling all right, you just squeeze my hand real hard and I'll squeeze right back to let you know I understand. O.K.?"

Melody and Mr. Nottoman found a comfortable spot on the fourth row before the crowd got there. Mr. Nottoman straightened a few bundles disarranged by the curious crowd and government grader. "No need to do that, Papa. Looks to me like those buyers tear it all to pieces anyway."

"Yes, but it's got to look nice to them before they'll even consider it."

"Look, Papa. They're here. Don't forget. Squeeze my hand real hard."

The auctioneer paused a minute and wiped his forehead. The crowd was almost still, and the buyers seemed to relax.

"What's the matter with them, Papa? Anything gone wrong?"

"Fifty-three cents," said the warehouseman.

"Fifty-four," shouted a buyer.

The auctioneer picked up the chant. Melody became lost in the mystery of his song.

"Papa, did you forget to squeeze?" said Melody at the end of the fourth pile.

"Goodness, child, I did. Forgive me," he said, as he squeezed Melody's hand real hard. Fifth pile, a squeeze, sixth pile, a hard squeeze, and on and on.

When the last pile was sold, Mr. Nottoman turned around, patted Melody on the shoulder, and started toward the office.

"It's all over but the check, now. Right, Papa? How did it really sell?"

"Very good except for the green and floor trash, and of course I didn't expect much for that."

"You know, Papa. I got worried about the hand-squeezing deal. All the time I kept saying to myself, 'I bet Papa is squeezing my hand just so I won't have a heart attack!' "

"Oh, Melody. I wouldn't deceive you. Not in the least of things. You know that. Now to the office for the check. That won't take long. The man in there can figure tickets and add figures faster than you can say John Henry."

"And then to see Mr. Ezra. Right, Papa? Where is Isaac?" Melody looked around. "Yonder he comes. He's probably kept up with us, but for a long time I didn't see him around here. I bet he's as anxious as we are to hear from Mr. Ezra."

Melody sat down on a bench outside the office to wait for Mr. Nottoman. She picked up a copy of the *Wilson Times.*

"Now I am dreaming. It can't be true; it can't be!"

She jumped up and moved toward the room where her father had gone to get the check for the tobacco.

"Papa might be mad if I go in there. Isaac! Isaac! Come here. Look at this."

"I can't read, Miss Melody. Gawd knows I can't. You can read. You read it to me."

"It says, 'Airport Not To Be Located in the Eastern Part of the County!' Look, Isaac. Look! That's what it says."

"I can't read, but I can hear real good, Miss Melody, an' I ain't never heard better news. Where is dey gonna put it?"

"Let's see. It doesn't say, Isaac."

Melody read on.

"It says that the location is still undecided, but it is certain that it won't be in our section."

"Thank Gawd. Thank Gawd. Dey ain't nowhere to live but at Big Oaks, nowhere in de whole world! Der comes Mr. Nottoman. Show it to him."

Melody handed the paper to her father. She watched his expression as he read. Then he reached out and took Melody's hand and squeezed it. It was the same kind of squeeze that he had given her when the tobacco sold "real good"; yet, this represented something more precious than money. It symbolized a joy that neither Melody nor her father nor Isaac nor anyone at Big Oaks would ever forget.

CHAPTER 15

"THIS IS THE CLEANEST PLACE I've ever seen, Papa," whispered Melody, as they walked down the corridors of the hospital. "These floors look like blue glass, and the nurses are so pretty."

"This is a good hospital," Mr. Nottoman agreed, nodding his head, "and Mr. Ezra is in good hands, I'm sure."

They stepped into an elevator. "Automatic, I see," Mr. Nottoman observed, as he pushed the third-floor button.

"I hate to act countrified, Papa, but this makes my stomach feel a little funny."

The elevator stopped, and the door opened. "Papa, I'm a little nervous. This day is just too much for me. Supposing Mr. Ezra isn't all right?"

"Don't you worry about that," her father assured her.

Outside the room they paused. Mr. Nottoman knocked gently. No one answered. He peeked through the little white curtain that extended from the top of the door to the bottom of the glass. Mr. Ezra was lying very still in his bed.

"Quiet, now. We just go in right quiet-like," said Mr. Nottoman. He went in and Melody followed. When Mr. Nottoman stood beside the bed, Mr. Ezra turned his head slightly to the left, away from him. Mr. Nottoman lifted his hand and placed it gently on the edge of the bed; and, for a moment, he just stood there.

Finally, he spoke. "How are you, Mr. Ezra?"

Mr. Ezra did not answer.

"You are better, I know. Melody and I are glad, Mr. Ezra."

Two big tears dropped from Mr. Ezra's weary eyes onto the bandage between his nose and mouth.

"You're going to be all right," Mr. Nottoman continued. "I know your burns hurt real bad, but you're going to be all right. We'll see you again soon, maybe tomorrow."

Mr. Nottoman took Melody's hand as he turned to leave, but Mr. Ezra moved.

"Don't go," he pleaded feebly. "Where is Isaac?"

"In the truck, Mr. Ezra," Mr. Nottoman answered.

"Did he get burned?"

"No. He's fine. Worried about you, of course."

"Will you shake his hand and thank him for me?"

"I will," replied Mr. Nottoman. "Is there anything else we can do for you?"

"Yes, yes. My lips are too sore to talk, Nottoman; but,

in case I die, there are a couple of things that need doing and saying."

"Now, you can wait on them until tomorrow. You'll feel much better then."

"No, they must be today. Some things just can't wait, you know." Mr. Ezra's voice was trembling and broken.

Mr. Nottoman nodded his head in understanding. "What is it then, Mr. Ezra?"

"Take that piece of paper there on the table and read it to Isaac. He's like me. He can't read it too good hisself, I don't reckon. Then give it to him and tell him it's all true, every word of it. Tell him my lawyer will make it all legal just as soon as possible." He paused to catch his breath. "I've been wrong about Isaac and Jake, as well as about a lot of other people. I know I talked ugly to them and accused them of things they would never have done, especially about stealing my corn this summer. I was wrong about that. Dead wrong. Will you tell them that for me?"

"We will, Mr. Ezra," said Mr. Nottoman. "We will be glad to."

After a few moments, Mr. Ezra spoke again between deep, labored breaths. "And . . . something else, Nottoman. One time, in anger, I said some ugly things about your Melody. But, she's really a fine young'un. I just wish my little girl had lived . . . maybe she would have turned out just like your Melody."

"Well, Mr. Ezra, thank you."

Melody reached over and took Mr. Ezra's hand gently. She would have liked to squeeze it as hard as she could. The big lump in her throat hurt when she swallowed. She felt as if she would burst into tears at any moment. "I thank you, too, Mr. Ezra, for those nice words."

"Melody? Is that you?" Mr. Ezra asked, turning his head more towards her.

"Yes, sir," she answered. She reached forward and lightly touched Mr. Ezra's fingers again.

Mr. Nottoman interrupted a moment, after looking at his watch. "Melody, I have to go check on the time for Little Moses' appointment tomorrow, but you can stay a few more minutes if Mr. Ezra feels up to it."

"Yes, please stay a few more minutes, Melody, and humor a poor, burned old man," Mr. Ezra pleaded.

"All right," she whispered. "I'll only stay a little while, Papa."

"Good-bye, Mr. Ezra. I'll see you again real soon," said Mr. Nottoman as he left the room, closing the door behind him.

Almost as soon as the door had closed behind Mr. Nottoman, someone knocked. Then, a young doctor came into the room, and his nurse followed.

"Good morning. This is my nurse, Miss Sills. I am Dr. Meyers, from Baltimore."

"How do you do," said Melody and Mr. Ezra almost simultaneously.

Melody turned to go outside to wait in the hall. Just as she did so, Dr. Meyers started telling Mr. Ezra that he was the eye, ear, nose, and throat specialist. When Melody heard the word *ear*, she turned around. Dr. Meyers had already noticed that she was leaving. "You don't have to leave, little lady. Miss Sills and I won't be long. We're just going to check Mr. Ezra's eyes and ears."

The nurse gently raised Mr. Ezra's head while Dr. Meyers carefully removed the bandages.

"Goodness!" thought Melody, clasping the palm of her hand over her mouth when she saw the blisters and red burns that covered Mr. Ezra's entire face and neck. "I wonder if he'll ever heal!" she said to herself.

As Dr. Meyers examined Mr. Ezra's head, Melody stood aside, overcome with compassion for Mr. Ezra. Yet, she was also desperately concerned about what Dr. Meyers could do for Teddy—Dr. Meyers, an ear specialist? Should she speak to him now? Should she wait and ask Papa? Was it proper to talk to a doctor without an appointment? Without paying him? But suppose he went downstairs and left town before she could ask him about Teddy. It might be a month before he came back or maybe never. This might be her only chance. But she must not do wrong or impose. After all, he was here to help poor, suffering Mr. Ezra.

Melody watched every move that Dr. Meyers made. He was short and stocky, with a natural dark tan. His hands were large but gentle. He was jolly, with a happy sound in his voice. Anybody could talk to him, she thought. He seemed always to smile slightly, yet there was a deep concern in his eyes. They, too, were dark, almost black; and his thick, black eyebrows almost met above his nose. When he looked at someone, he did it with a kind of squinch that made little wrinkles on each side of his eyes and in his forehead. His thick, black hair was cut short, but there was a hint of uncontrolled curl that no amount of cutting could hide completely.

Dr. Meyers examined Mr. Ezra mostly through questions, since the blisters interfered with complete examination. He assured Mr. Ezra that he would keep a close check on him to be sure that any complications that arose would be given immediate attention. Miss Sills replaced the bandages with the doctor's help.

Turning to go, he paused to speak to Melody.

"You're mighty pretty—and mighty considerate to come to see Mr. Ezra. I know you are a ray of sunshine to him."

"Thank you, Dr. Meyers. He's lucky to have a good doctor."

"And thank you," he said, as he walked towards the door. "I'll be back to see Mr. Ezra, and if I can ever help you, let me know."

"Well, I tell you what," she said, following him into the hallway. "No, that's all right. I'll tell you later—maybe!"

"Oh, come now. What goes? Do you have a problem now?"

Melody felt that she could not turn down this opportunity.

"Well, if you have just a minute, I do have a problem. It's about my little brother, Teddy, who is four years old. He has a deformed ear; in fact, he has no ear at all." Then Melody related the whole story to Dr. Meyers, concerning Teddy's ear and the worry and heartache it had caused her and her parents. "Will he ever, by a miracle, have an ear?" she asked.

Dr. Meyers smiled. "You're quite a girl, Melody. You have described a big problem, but much research has been done and progress has been made in this area. Through recent advances in plastic surgery, we've seen miracles. We're even experimenting with the growing of real ears by transplanting human flesh."

Melody lifted her hands to her face. She lowered

them and looked for a second at Dr. Meyers. Suddenly, she dropped her head and buried her face in her hands.

"There now. What goes? Why all the tears?"

"Your words are a miracle. This is the greatest thing that will ever happen to me." Melody was quiet for a moment. Then she asked, "But how much will it cost?"

"Oh, we'll talk about that later, maybe with your father, if he wishes to discuss it."

"He will. I know he will. But I must know what it will cost."

"Naturally, these things run into hundreds of dollars. Treatment and operations must be gradual, a little each year. But don't worry about it. We'll see about that after I talk to your father and after I see Teddy."

"Papa and I can talk to you this morning, if you're going to be here in the hospital for a while."

"That's fine. Let's see. In about half an hour I'll be in Dr. Beddard's office. You all just stop by if you want to."

Melody started to reach forth her hand for a handshake, but instead she threw both arms around Dr. Meyers, laid her face against his chest, and between the choking tears said, "Thank you, Dr. Meyers. Thank you with all my heart."

"You're welcome, Melody. And I'll see you and your father downstairs in half an hour." Dr. Meyers patted her gently on the back. Then he and the nurse walked off down the hall.

Suddenly, Melody remembered that she had promised to meet her father in the lobby. She quickly stuck her head back into Mr. Ezra's room, since the door was still ajar. "I really hate to go, Mr. Ezra, but I've got to meet Papa. I'll be back tomorrow, though. Papa or Buster will bring me. I know they will. And we're going to bring Mrs. Ezra. She's doing fine, but she's still a little tired from the fire and mighty worried about you."

"You're a little girl, Melody. But you talk like a woman—a real fine, good woman."

"Thank you, Mr. Ezra."

"You're welcome, Melody. And I mean every word of it." Mr. Ezra was quiet and thoughtful for a moment. Then he continued. "During the fire, Melody, I had already give up to die. Then I heard your voice. I knew you had found a way to me. I knew I was saved. Later, I heard about all you did. You and Isaac." He paused again to catch his breath. "I gave your Pa a note for Isaac before he left. That note gives him something he wants awful bad, something any man who lives off the land would want. And . . . and, now, I want to do something good and important for you."

Melody stood beside Mr. Ezra's bed now. She did not know when she had walked across the room. She was surprised. Speechless. She had not expected any reward for helping a man in trouble. Finally, she was able to say, "Mr. Ezra, I thank you for the thought, but you don't have to give me anything. . . ."

"I know, child." He coughed. "It's because I want to . . . I never wanted to give nothing to nobody before in my life. But, I want to do something for you that I know will make you happy. You'll be happier about this than if it was something for you directly."

Melody was stunned, puzzled. She could not imagine what Mr. Ezra meant.

"I heard you talking in the hall with Dr. Meyers. What I want to do is pay for Teddy's doctor bills and hospital bills." He paused again. He was getting very tired and was coughing more than before.

"Oh, Mr. Ezra. Thank you. Thank you again and again. I will try to be worthy of your goodness. With all my heart, I promise." She felt the hot tears welling up in her eyes. "Nothing could make me any happier than what you have just told me."

"I know, Melody. I know. Nothing I could have given you would have been half as good as a little help for your brother. I'm just glad I can offer that help. It does a mean old man like me a lot of good to know you are happy and free of that big worry you've been carrying around for so long."

They were both quiet for a few moments, as Melody dried her tears and squeezed Mr. Ezra's hand as much as she dared. Finally, he said with a smile in his voice,

"Now, you go on down and tell your Pa . . . and then go see Dr. Meyers. Everything's gonna be all right."

"Oh, yes, Mr. Ezra. Everything will be all right now. And thank you so very much. I'll never be able to thank you enough."

When Melody got downstairs, Mr. Nottoman was waiting in the lobby.

"Am I late, Papa? I'm sorry. But I know two wonderful things to tell you, the most wonderful things I've ever known, and that's why I'm late," Melody said, as Mr. Nottoman turned to the door to leave. "Please, Papa, wait just a minute and I'll tell you."

Then she excitedly told him about her talk with Dr. Meyers and about Mr. Ezra's gift to her. "He said he would pay all the bills for Teddy. And he seemed to be so happy about it, Papa."

"That really is good news, Melody. And it's mighty good and generous of Mr. Ezra."

"The doctor is waiting in Dr. Beddard's office for us to talk with him. Can we, Papa?"

"Of course, Melody. Of course." Mr. Nottoman smiled and put his arm around her shoulders.

Before they left the hospital, Mr. Nottoman and Melody talked in detail with the doctor, who offered to see Teddy the next Thursday. That would be fine, Mr. Nottoman said. They could bring Teddy when they came

141

to bring Little Moses to have his bandages removed.

Isaac was waiting in the truck for them. It was hot, and he was perspiring.

"Mr. Ezra sure is strange looking," Melody told Isaac as soon as they got in the truck. "He's all bandaged from head to foot and all the human being you can see is his eyes, his nose hole, and his mouth. And, I saw his burns when the doctor came. He's a pitiful sight."

"You think he'll live, Miss Melody?"

"Oh, yes. And he's going to be a changed man and a better neighbor. You just wait and see."

"And he especially wanted us to thank you for last night, Isaac," Mr. Nottoman said. "He sure is grateful to you."

"He's mighty welcome. Mighty welcome," said Isaac, with tears in his eyes.

"And," Mr. Nottoman continued, "he said for me to give you this paper, but I'm supposed to read it to you first, according to Mr. Ezra's request."

Issac nodded his head. His eyes stared straight ahead. The note was written in a nurse's neat handwriting, followed by Mr. Ezra's shaky signature. Mr. Nottoman read:

"I, Ezra Bowles, give to Isaac Binger, son of Alice-Cora-Jane and Jake Binger, the one acre of land that lies beside the creek next to Mr. Nottoman's land. He may use it for planting corn or for a garden or for building a house, or in any other way he chooses. I will instruct my lawyer to draw the deed as soon as possible.

Ezra Bowles"

Mr. Nottoman handed the paper to Isaac.

"Oh, Isaac," Melody squealed. "He said it was something good, and it is!"

"I can't take it, Miss Melody. Gawd knows I can't. He don't owe me nothin'. Ain't right to take pay for helpin' a pore burnin' man. Anybody coulda' and shoulda' did the same."

"We understand how you feel, Isaac," agreed Mr. Nottoman. "But, it's yours. He is giving it to you, straight out. It would make him feel bad if you didn't take it."

Melody knew that her father was thinking about Mr. Ezra's offer to help Teddy.

As Mr. Nottoman drove homeward, they were all silent. Melody was lost in a flood of memories. It seemed only yesterday that she and her father had sat on the front porch and talked about Teddy's problem and shared the hopelessness of the situation. But now it was different, and all because of Mr. Ezra.

"You know something, Papa," Melody said, as they left the city limits of Wilson and headed down the asphalt road toward Big Oaks. "Those were strange things that Mr. Ezra said and did today, weren't they?"

"Yes, they were. He's a changed man, I believe."

"But, why, Papa? Why did he have to get burned almost to death to think those nice things he said about colored folks and other people and all?"

"I don't know, Melody. Life is strange. The Good Master teaches us and speaks to us in many ways. Maybe His dealings with Mr. Ezra are like my work in the spring when I go out into the field and take Rodie and Kate and start to break land. If I waited until April and just smoothed the land and tried to make rows, I'd have nothing but hard, stubborn earth, full of rubbish and stalks and leaves and everything. That won't work. First the land has to be broken, slowly and deep, so that it can air out and the soft spring rains can soak in. Then we can go out and do almost anything we want to with the land."

"Oh, you mean Mr. Ezra is like broken acres of land."

"Maybe, in a way. We're not the Judge. But we can observe and maybe gather something good for our lives." Mr. Nottoman put his arm around Melody. "You're a sleepy girl. Just look at your eyes. They're bloodshot. It's been a long day."

"And a long night," added Melody.

"Tomorrow I have to bring Little Moses back to the hospital to have his bandages changed. In all the excitement, I had almost forgotten," said Mr. Nottoman.

"And I'd like to come back to see Mr. Ezra and bring

Mrs. Ezra. I had thought of sleeping late, but I guess, if I really look at it right, I can sleep plenty of mornings when there's nothing better to do."